COTTONWOOD PASS

Books by Chance Cooper:

McCart Series:
Logan's Vengeance (1st Book)
Cottonwood Pass   (2nd Book)

Other Books:
Coming Soon:
Montana Skirts

Many thanks to my friends who have provided me encouragement, and meaningful feedback to assist me in my writing.

Special thanks to Linda Rails for her help with editing.

Cottonwood Pass

It isn't enough that Logan has to contend with Bart Hickey, a dangerous claim jumper trying to kill him. Now Quentin Bellows, the older brother of the man who murdered Logan's parents, and who Logan killed, has joined forces with Hickey.

Logan pulled his revolver and checked the loads. He pushed Clady aside and started toward the saloon. Stepping inside he saw Bellows sitting at a table toward the back. "Stand up Bellows, this ends here."

Cottonwood Pass

Written By
Chance Cooper

Published by: Books By Chance

ISBN-13: 978-0615951041

.

Chapter 1

At the close of the Civil War, Nathan and Emily McCart were murdered by Missouri Ruffian Jim Bellows. Bellows lead a gang of forty ruffians and murdered the McCart's to claim the Circle M cattle ranch, located in west Kansas. What he hadn't counted on was the capability and determination of the McCart children, twins Logan and Lisa McCart. At the time of their parents death, Logan was a Major in the Union Army stationed in Southern Virginia, and Lisa was attending Columbia University in New York City.

Bellows hired an old friend, Ben Stiles, who had opened a detective agency in New York to cover for his criminal activities of murder and blackmail, to find and kill the McCart children. Bellows wanted to eliminate any family members who could mount a challenge to his ownership of the Circle M ranch, and disrupt his plans of becoming a respected cattleman. Aside from Bellows attempts to hire out the killings to Stiles, and other paid killers, he and his forty men were unable to kill the twins and keep the ranch.

Only twenty two years old at the end of the war, Logan had honed his survival skills through his childhood upbringing, playing and hunting with the Cheyenne and Arapaho Indians. Serving four years in the Union Army enhanced those skills. While the odds were with Bellows, he and his men were no match for Logan McCart.[1]

---

[1] Logan's Vengeance

Logan and Lisa are both very intelligent. Not surprising since their father was a well educated man from England, and their mother was a school teacher from Pennsylvania. Logan is a fair and compassionate man, something instilled in him by his kind and loving parents. However, he has no tolerance for those who harm, or prey on the weak and old.

In exacting his vengeance for his parent's death, Logan offered every one of Bellows men the opportunity to lay down their arms and live. Only one of Bellows men, Joey, took the offer and survived. No such accommodation was given Bellows himself.

It is now the spring of 1868, and it has been slightly more than two years since Logan killed Jim Bellows, avenging his parents' murder and reclaiming the family ranch. Although his skill with all kinds of weapons provided him the opportunity to overcome such odds, it was his service in the army, during the civil war, that taught him how to kill his fellow man. Up until the war he had only used his skills against the wildlife he hunted.

There hasn't been any further trouble from land grabbers, or any indication of retribution by anyone that had known or was loyal to Bellows. Logan was unaware that Bellows had an older brother being held in a Federal Prison in Missouri.

Logan was riding the far pastures of the ranch, evaluating the strength and health of the herd when his mind began to wander. I can't believe how fast the last two years have flown by.

Working the ranch with my sister Lisa has allowed me to put Bellows behind me for the most part.

Lisa seems happy now that she is engaged to Greg Stevenson, the family lawyer. At 35,000 acres and the herd back up to 10,000 head, I really haven't had time to think much about anything else but the ranch itself. Except for on Sundays, when Lisa and I would visit our parents graves.

Greg is the primary partner of the Stevenson and Son Law Firm. The firm was established in 1830, in Indiana, and moved to Lawrence Kansas in 1860. Greg's father had been retained by our father, Nathan McCart, back in 1832. After Greg's engagement to Lisa, he opened a second law office in Junction City, and now lives there so he can be closer to her.

Peace has broken down between the Indians and the Army. However, Logan is a blood brother to the Cheyenne and Arapaho, and he continues to honor his father's original pact with the tribes to provide them beef. In return, the tribes provide the Circle M protection.

A lone rider crested the hill and was riding straight for Logan. Snapping out of his daydreaming, Logan rode over to greet the rider. It was Grey Wolf, Chief of the Arapaho Nation. "Greetings Grey Wolf, what brings you over this way?"

"Greetings Logan. The buffalo are few, and my people are in need of food and blankets. My braves said they saw you out here alone, and riding without purpose. What weighs on your mind my brother?"

"I was just enjoying the peace and quiet, and thinking of times past. I think maybe it's time for me to go on that hunting trip I have been planning all winter. Now that things are stable, and the ranch is operating efficiently, I could use a little solitude up in the mountains for some much needed relaxation."

"You want that the Arapaho keep an eye on your sister and the ranch while you are gone?"

"Thanks Grey Wolf, but she will be fine with the others at the ranch. I am sorry the peace has been broken, and that they are killing all the buffalo. I will have Randy bring you some cattle. If you need anything else, like grain, while I'm gone, just send word to Randy. He will make sure you get whatever you need."

"Your family has always been a great friend to the Arapaho and Cheyenne. We will never forget." Saying goodbye, Grey Wolf rode back to his lodge.

After his battle with Bellows and his men, Logan had never really had any time to wash it all away. He and Lisa immediately started getting the ranch back up and running. And while his sister had Greg as a release, and time away from the ranch, Logan has not had any real solitude to heal emotionally.

While riding back to the ranch house he returned to his thoughts of traveling. With Greg, Randy, and Joey all around to protect Lisa, and help her run the ranch, he feels comfortable enough to leave the ranch for an extended period of time.

Thanks to his father's vision, and the courage to carve out a living in the untamed and desolate unorganized territory back in the early 30's, Logan and Lisa are worth well over a million dollars. As new comers arrived to build a new life in the territory, their father helped them with cash or livestock, sometimes both, to help establish themselves. In return he accepted a percentage of ownership of their businesses and ranches. Those holdings now belong to Lisa and Logan. Not to mention their own ranch, which is one of the largest, if not the largest, in the territory.

Bellows and his fellow ruffians all had wanted posters on them for one crime or another. As a result, Logan was awarded $10,000 in bounty money. But it also gave him the unwanted reputation of being fast with a gun. Unless you are a lawman or professional gunfighter, it's not the type of reputation you want. Having such a reputation can only bring trouble. If some relative or associate of the men you kill is not tracking you down to settle the score, some young gun is hunting you to make a name for himself.

Logan usually traveled under his alias, "Logan Hayes", when not conducting ranch business, mainly to disassociate his exploits as Logan McCart that might bring him, or the ranch, unwanted trouble. He first assumed his alias in New York, when he used it to help him save his sister from ben Stiles, a man Bellows had hired to kill her, and himself.

For the next couple of days Logan finished his personal work around the ranch and prepared to leave. Randy cut out twenty five head of prime beef and drove them over to Grey Wolf's encampment as requested by Logan.

The time had come for Logan to go on his hunting trip. "Randy, have all the ranch hands gather in the yard outside the main house." Randy had worked for Logan's father, and aided Logan in his fight against Bellows. Whenever Logan requested something he did it without question. After the last man had arrived, Randy went up to the house and notified Logan everyone was present.

Logan stepped out on the front porch. "Good morning men. I want to thank you all for your hard work over these past two years. The herd is large enough again to make a drive and sell off half the herd. I am going to be gone for most of the summer. Now that spring is coming to a close I want you to brand the young stuff and cull the herd. Stage the culled herd in the northern pastures. Randy is still foreman and will be in charge during my absence. I expect you to follow his orders without question. Shortly after my return we will make the cattle drive to Wichita. That's all men, Randy, you and Joey remain behind. I would like to talk to you two separately."

"Joey, I expect you to protect the ranch, and help Randy out all you can. I especially want you to stay close to the house and pro Lisa while I'm gone. Randy is a good foreman and a trusted friend, but he is getting up in age, and he has no skill with a gun, unless it's that Greener shotgun of his." Randy blew a snort in disgust at the remark, but he knew it was true. Logan just smiled at him and returned his attention to Joey. "Joey, you have proven yourself to be a loyal hand, and a trusted friend since my fight against Bellows. Do you have any questions, or need anything before I leave?"

Joey had been a part of Bellows gang, and never understood why Logan had hired him on. So he took this opportunity to ask him. "Mr. McCart, I never really thanked you for allowing me to leave the ranch alive after Bellows killed your parents, and stole your ranch. If you don't mind my asking, what made you decide to hire me, instead of killing me when I rode up on one of your horses looking for a job? You had to know who I was."

"I spoke with Marshall Brodie before he left the ranch and returned to Lawrence, Joey. He told me of his conversation with you at the café in Junction City. I am sure you remember it, it was just before he was forced to kill Pete and Glenn at the saloon. He said he believed you when you told him you wanted to go straight, and were looking for honest work. He asked me to hire you if you ever showed up looking for a job as a favor to him."

"Thank you sir, first you gave me the chance to live, and then you gave me a job and a place to call home. You will never regret it, and I won't let you down."

"I know you won't Joey. Just make sure you take care of my sister and Randy while I'm gone."

Joey walked away and Logan turned his attention to Randy. "Randy, can you catch up Blue and Sallie for me?"

Randy was somewhat surprised when Logan requested Sallie. "Boss, I can understand you takin' the blue roan, but Sallie, you know how cantankerous she can get."

"Might be, but she is the best pack mule we have. And with those long legs she is better equipped for climbing around the Rockies than any horse we have. Besides, she has been traveling the back pastures of the ranch with me for two years now, and she follows me without having to keep her on a lead rope."

"Do you want me to saddle Dusty for you?" Randy asked, knowing the answer before he asked.

"No, I will saddle Dusty and pack all the supplies. Put the sawbuck pack saddles on Blue and Sallie, and then bring them around to the front corral. Tie them up next to Dusty for me, and I'll load the packs."

I had already saddled Dusty and slid my Henry repeater into its boot when Randy brought Blue and Sallie around. After checking the cinches of the pack saddles, I put my saddle holster, which carried a LeMat revolver, over my saddle horn.

The LeMat is a gun that was used primarily by the soldiers in the southern army. Logan had admired the weapon and bought one for himself to use in his fight against Bellows. It saved his life on two occasions, and has become a favorite of his to travel with.

The LeMat is known for its versatility. It has a pistol cylinder that holds nine.44 caliber shots that rotates over a single shot 16 gauge shotgun barrel. There is a switch on the hammer that changes it to fire from one barrel to the other.

The last weapon he packed was his father's old Hawken, a.54 caliber musket rifle. It is now over thirty years old, but it's still in great condition, and Logan loves hunting with it, as opposed to his Henry repeater. The Hawken has an effective killing range of 400 hundred yards. Which is a hundred yards less than the newer Sharps breach loading rifle. But it has the same maximum range of 1,000 yards as the Sharps.

He put the extra shot and powder for the Hawken in the pouch of the saddle holster. After he finished loading his supplies he kissed Lisa on the cheek, and said goodbye to her, Randy and Joey, as he rode out for Cottonwood Pass.

No matter how safe he believed things at the ranch were, there was still that doubt in his mind as to whether he was doing the right thing by leaving them, and if they would be okay without his protection.

Chapter 2

I crossed the Arkansas River just behind the ranch house, and headed my horses west along the Santa Fe Trail. The trail follows the Arkansas River west all the way to the base of the Rocky Mountains, then heads south to Santa Fe, while the river turns north.

It was not long after I entered the trail that I noticed the tracks of two wagons traveling ahead of me. Based on the piles left by the mules pulling the wagons, they appeared to be approximately an hour in front of me. Those wagons would not cover more than three miles an hour. I figure at that pace I should catch up with them around dusk. With any luck they will invite me to dinner so I won't have to eat my own cooking. Those pioneer women are some of the best cooks you'll ever find.

My thoughts were drifting towards the mountains as I rode lazily in the saddle. I hadn't been on the trail much more than an hour when I came across the tracks of three riders leading a pack mule. They entered the trail from the north, telling me that they had crossed the ranch through Cheyenne territory. Based on the tracks, they were now between me and the wagons. The pack mule was heavily loaded, probably with buffalo hides, and it was apparent that they were not traveling with the wagons further ahead.

It could be that we are all headed in the same direction, but I didn't like the look of it. Logan spurred Dusty into a trot to close the distance between himself and the wagons. Blue was tied to Sallie, and although they fell behind, Sallie kept following Dusty's scent as usual. She would catch up later as she had done on so many other occasions.

The three buffalo hunters rode up softly and caught the wagons by surprise. As they rode up beside the wagons, the one leading the mule slowed and rode abreast of the second wagon. He kept the young driver covered with his rifle. The other two rode forward and the leader caught up the reigns of the mules, and pulled the lead wagon to an abrupt halt. The buffalo hunters knew most pioneers carried a cash box with all their money and family valuables in it. And this group looked like easy pickings.

The man holding the mules harness turned his attention back to the wagon. "Hello there folks, my name is Amos Curry. Where y'all headed?"

The man driving the lead wagon did the talking. "My name is Ben Nelson. We are from Indiana, and are on our way to California."

"You're a little too far south if you're headed to the California gold mines."

"We are farmers. We have no interest in searching for gold. I would appreciate it if you would let go of the trace lines on my mules so we can be on our way."

Curry spat a mouth full of tobacco into the dirt as he gave Mr. Nelson a surly look. "Well that's not very hospitable of you. I don't think I like your attitude. Set the brake on that wagon Mr. Nelson, and everyone step down off both wagons."

"We don't want any trouble mister, we just want to go on about our way."

"I don't care what you want, now get down before I blast you off that seat."

Amos Curry and his partners were a foul looking and smelling bunch. Fearful for their lives, Mr. Nelson instructed his family to get down from the wagons. He knew he couldn't stop them. But he figured if he just let them take what they wanted without any resistance, that they would most likely leave without harming anyone.

I pulled off the trail and dismounted behind a small knoll. It didn't take me long to figure out the pioneers were being robbed. I raised my rifle and tucked it up into my shoulder. I wanted to be ready to fire if need be. It wouldn't have been anything for me to kill all three of those filthy hunters before they even laid a hand on their weapons. But they haven't done anything to die for just yet, at least not that I knew about. I decided to wait and see how things played out before taking a hand in the matter.

"Quint, you and Zak get up in those wagons and find their money box, and search for anything else worth taking, like jewelry."

Quint was up in the first wagon rummaging around when he yelled out. "Amos, they got a couple rifles in here, you want them too?"

"Yeah, they won't have any need for them where they're going."

Mr. Nelson knew they would not survive in the wilderness without those rifles. Without thinking he blurted out. "We need those rifles to hunt for food, and for protection against the Indians."

"Shut up Nelson, I'm not going to tell you again to keep your trap closed."

It was now obvious to Logan that the men meant to kill the pioneers. Quint and Zak were throwing all the family belongings out of the wagons onto the trail when they heard the rifle shot. Quint poked his head out of the lead wagon, and asked, "Amos, who did you shoot?"

"It wasn't me who shot, somebody shot me in the shoulder."

"Those pilgrims aren't holding any weapons Amos, who shot you?"

"I don't know you idiot. The shot came from behind that knoll over there."

Just then they heard a strange man yelling to them from behind the knoll. "You two, in the wagons, get out and drop your weapons."

It was Zak who asked the question. "Amos, what do we do?"

"Do as he tells you. He has us covered and we can't see him." Quint and Zak did as they were told. After dropping their weapons they climbed out of the wagons.

Still hidden behind the knoll, Logan shouted out again. "Now, you three scalawags start walking to the rear of the wagons toward me, and don't stop until I tell you." The three started walking back in the direction of the knoll, still unaware of who, or how many were out there. Logan remained out of sight until they were well past the wagons. "That's far enough, now lay face down in the dirt."

Confused as to who was out there, Amos shouted over to the knoll. "Who are you?"

"You will find out soon enough. Now get face down in the dirt before I shoot you in the knees, and make you fall down." The three men did as they were told. "Now stretch your arms out in front over your heads. And I better not see any weapons in them." After doing as they were told, Logan stepped out from behind the knoll leading Dusty. Sallie followed with Blue attached. She had caught up and sidled up next to Dusty while Logan had been watching what was happening at the wagons. Walking towards them, Logan spoke to the man who seemed to be in charge of the wagons. "You, the leader of the wagons, what is your name?"

"Ben Nelson."

"Mr. Nelson, come over here and check them for guns and knives. Make sure you approach them from behind, and don't come between them and me. Make sure you check their boots for any hide away weapons."

Mr. Nelson did as he was instructed. He didn't know who this stranger was, but since he was helping them, he was not going to argue.

"After you search them for weapons step back to your family." Logan walked up to the men laying in the dirt. "Whew, you three stink, why didn't you stop and bathe when you crossed the Arkansas River? I see your mule there is loaded down with buffalo hides, did you get those on the Cheyenne lands?"

"What of it, you an Indian lover or something?"

"Actually, I am blood brother to the Chief of the Cheyenne Dog Soldiers. "Ben, check in their side packs and see if you can find some leather bindings." After finding some, Logan instructed him to tie their hands and feet. Once again Ben Nelson did as he was told. "Good, now let's walk back to your wagons Mr. Nelson."

Ben Nelson was curious as to what Logan's intentions were for the three thieves. "What about them?"

"They are not going anywhere." Logan tipped his hat, "Good afternoon ma'am, my name is Logan Hayes."

"Good Afternoon sir. Thank you for your help, I was afraid they were going to kill us."

"Well, they aren't going to harm anyone now ma'am. Mr. Nelson, have your son pull that rear wagon alongside the lead wagon to make a box camp. Tell him to leave enough space in between the wagons for us to make a good fire without setting the canvas on fire, and so we'll have plenty of room to lay out our sleeping gear. Then have him grab the ropes off those men's saddles, and connect them from one wagon to the other for a hitch line to tie the horses and mules. I know it's a bit early to stop and camp for the night, but we have to wait here for some friends of mine. In the meantime we can talk about the hardships that lay ahead of you."

Mr. Nelson suddenly felt threatened again, and inquired sharply. "Friends, did you save us from that scum only to rob us yourself after your friends arrive?"

"Nothing like that Mr. Nelson. I am on your side, and my friends will be coming to collect those three fellows tied up over there in the dirt. I don't know if you noticed it or not, but they have a female Indian scalp hanging off those hides. And if I am right, there will be a party of Cheyenne Dog Soldiers riding up pretty soon."

Once again, Mr. Nelson's face showed fear. "Indians, why aren't we preparing to defend ourselves instead of sitting around talking?"

"I told you, they are friends of mine. I don't know if you heard me tell that Amos character or not, but I am a blood brother to their Chief, so you have no reason to be alarmed or frightened. When they ride in have your family stay calm, and whatever you do, don't anyone grab for a weapon."

"We will do as you say Mr. Hayes. I guess we can trust you, after all you did save us from a terrible fate at the hands of those men." Mr. Nelson relayed the instructions for everyone to stay in the camp, and to. do as Mr. Hayes had instructed them.

Just before dusk the Chief of the Cheyenne Dog Soldiers, along with a dozen Braves, rode up to their camp. Logan stepped out with his hand raised and open. "Hello Running Elk." The Nelson's all huddled together. No matter what assurances Logan had given them, they still were not sure if the Indians could be trusted, and they were fearful of being killed by savage Indians.

Running Elk was surprised to see Logan. "Hello my brother, I wasn't expecting to see you. We are tracking three killers of my people."

"The three men you are looking for are laying over there face down and tied up."

"Who are these pilgrims you sit with?"

"Just a pioneer family moving west to California, a place over the mountains. Those three were robbing them, and getting ready to kill them when I rode up. I would appreciate it if you treated these folks as if they were my own family."

"Very well, we will make sure they remain safe until they reach the mountains."

While the Braves loaded the three hunters belly down across their saddles, and tied their hands and feet together under the horses' bellies, Logan retrieved their mule with the skins and handed it over to Running Elk. "Logan, where are you headed?"

"I am going up to Cottonwood Pass to hunt Elk. Why don't you join me?"

"I wish I could, but we are having trouble with the pioneers, and buffalo hunters such as these. Good hunting my brother, come sit with me when you get back."

"I will. Say hello to Grey Wolf for me, and let him know I have gone on that hunt I spoke to him about."

Waving goodbye the Cheyenne rode out with the three hunters in tow. Running Elk had four of his warriors hang back to follow the pioneers from a distance. They were to keep watch over the pioneers until they reached the base of the mountains.

"Mr. Hayes, what will the Indians do to those men?"

"You don't need to concern yourself with that Mr. Nelson. Just know whatever they do, those men have earned every bit of it for killing one of their squaws. And most likely would have killed you and your family had I not come along."

"What do we do with their weapons?"

"Keep them or sell them. The choice is yours since they belong to you now."

"Mr. Hayes do you think we might hire you on as a guide to take us through to California?"

"Thanks for the offer Mr. Nelson, but I am headed north, and I don't have any interest in being a guide. I will be leaving you where the Mountain and Cimarron Routes of the Santa Fe Trail split. That is where you will leave the Arkansas River and continue south. I will ride with you until we reach the split. After that the Cheyenne will make sure you remain safe until you get to the Sangre De Cristo Mountain Range. Then you will be back on your own."

"Does that mean they will be riding alongside our wagons?"

"No, you will not see them, but they will be watching, and will come to your aide if you run into trouble."

That night they talked long into the evening around the fire. Logan provided them with many tips on how to protect themselves, and suggested they hook up with a wagon train in Santa Fe for the remainder of their trip to California. He advised them that if they continued on alone, they would be more vulnerable to highway men and attacks from the Kiowa and Comanche tribes, than if they were traveling in a group.

Logan admired the spirit of the pioneer. But they were like all other manner of God's creations, some were better suited for the life than others.

Most pioneers made the journey because they just couldn't make a living back east. Others did it for the adventure, or to seek riches. Whatever the reason, many died along the trail in their efforts to make a new life.

Chapter 3

Running Elk took the three buffalo hunters back to the Cheyenne's main camp. The squaw they had raped, killed and scalped, was the wife of one of the lower chiefs. After stripping the three men down, they were tied up to posts in the middle of a fire pit. For three days they were beaten with sticks and rocks by the women and children. They were given just enough water to remain alive. The next two days the braves used their hunting knifes to make cuts all over their bodies. They were careful not to cut all the way through the skin and cause them to bleed to death. The cuts were numerous and very painful, and the blood that oozed out caused biting flies to swarm them. On the sixth day they were scalped and castrated. Shortly thereafter, while they were still conscious, they were burned at the stake.

Logan left the Nelson's where the Santa Fe Trail split. He headed northwest along the Mountain Route of the trail that followed the Arkansas River. The Nelson's continued south along the Cimarron Route. They would be safe until they reached the Sangre De Cristo mountain range with Running Elk's braves keeping watch over them. From there it was only a short distance to Santa Fe. If they don't sign on with a wagon train at Santa Fe, Logan doesn't believe they will live to make it to California.

A day later, Logan rode into what used to be the Big Timbers trading post. The post was isolated and showed signs that it had been destroyed by a flood. He had visited this trading post back in the fifties while hunting buffalo with James "Pearl" Brodie. He was only fifteen at the time, and Brodie was in his late twenties. Brodie is now a U. S. Federal Marshall living in Lawrence, Kansas.

Big Timbers trading post was established after the original post, Bent's Old Fort trading post, was abandoned after the cholera epidemic in 1849, and burnt to the ground by William Bent. Bent's Old Fort was re-established farther west. Although named a fort, it was really only a trading post built to trade with trappers, and the Southern Cheyenne and Arapaho tribes for buffalo robes. For much of its 16-year history, it was the only major permanent settlement on the Santa Fe Trail between Missouri and the Mexican settlements.

I unsaddled my horses, gave them a good rub down, and fed them some grain before leading them down into the river to soothe their legs and fill their bellies with water. After setting up camp I scouted around to see if any other travelers had passed through lately. It didn't take long before I found the tracks of five men riding light and fast. Based on their camp fire, they are riding about two days ahead of me. The horses are shod, so that pretty much ruled them out as being Indians. One of the horses had a slight groove in its right rear shoe print. The lead horse had a star design imprinted in its front shoe. Probably a signature of the blacksmith that shoed the horse.

The next day, while enjoying my morning coffee, I was visited by a Cheyenne hunting party. Having grown up with the Cheyenne I speak their language very well. They told me of seeing the five riders ahead of me, and let me know they were heavily armed, but weren't hunting buffalo. After the Indians left I struck camp and headed towards Las Animas and Fort Lyon.

About a mile outside the town of Las Animas I saw the fort sitting off the trail to the north. A cold beer would have to wait, figuring the army would know of any trouble in the area, I decided to ride to the fort first. As I entered the Commanding Officer's office I received a pleasant surprise. The Commanding Officer was an old friend of mine from the Civil War.

Upon seeing Logan enter, the Commander gave him a hearty greeting. "Logan McCart, how are you doing my friend?"

"Very well, thank you. It is really good to see you Major Chaffey."

"Please, call me Jim. We have been friends too long to stand on ceremony."

"Okay, Jim, and just so you know, I am traveling under my alias of Logan Hayes."

"Logan, I was really sorry to hear about the murder of your parents. It was my understanding that you wiped out the Bellows gang. Why are you using your alias, you aren't out hunting bounty are you?"

"You are right about my business with the Bellows gang being over. I finished that two years ago. I'm headed up to Cottonwood Pass to hunt Elk. I like to travel under my alias when not on ranch business. So if trouble does find me it doesn't find its way back to the ranch."

"Very well then, if anyone asks, I will be sure to refer to you as Mr. Hayes."

"Jim, is there any trouble brewing around these parts I should know about?"

"Not locally, but there has been a large gold discovery up at Tin Cup. Lots of people headed that way, especially since the Pueblo mines have played out. Some good people are up there, but also some not so good. There have already been some killings up around St. Elmo and the Monarch Pass. It appears someone is killing and robbing the miners of their fortune as they are headed back down to the plains. If I was you I'd stay clear of Tin Cup."

"Good advice. I'm not hunting gold so I think I'll skirt around the mines, and go farther up into the northern range of the pass."

"Logan, I also got word about some buffalo hunters that went afoul of the Cheyenne. Anything you might be able to tell me about that?"

"It just so happens Jim, that I came upon those three hunters robbing some pioneers from Indiana. I intervened, but I didn't kill them. After I had them tied up I saw a Cheyenne scalp hanging off their bundle of hides. Turns out they raped and killed a Cheyenne squaw, then scalped her. They did it while hunting buffalo on Cheyenne land. I turned them over to Running Elk. If I was you I wouldn't concern myself with them."

"Very well, I trust your judgment, and I'll consider the matter closed."

"Thanks. Jim, I have been riding behind five riders since leaving Big Timbers. They seem to be traveling light and fast. I know they came through here and thought maybe you could tell me something about them?"

"Some of my men mentioned seeing five toughs in the Las Animas saloon a couple days ago. Said they picked up some conversation about them heading up to Tin Cup. I doubt they are miners, if I had to guess I would say they are claim jumpers."

"You're just full of good news aren't you. Thanks for the information, and I'll try and keep clear of trouble." Logan said goodbye and headed into town.

Chapter 4

After stabling my horses down at the livery stable, I got a room over at the hotel for the night and stored my gear. Wanting to wet the dryness gripping my throat, I walked over to Crazy Annies saloon for a cold beer. Besides wanting a drink, the saloon was always the best place to catch up on the local gossip. I was standing at the bar enjoying a cold beer, when two men walked in and stepped up beside me. After ordering their drinks, they began to talk about the event that took place three nights before.

"Emmitt, I am telling you that was Bart Hickey that drew on those two soldiers the other night."

"C'mon Warren, he wouldn't dare show his face around these parts after that trouble in Pueblo back in the late 50's."

"Emmitt, I'm willing to bet he's headed up to Tin Cup to jump those claims. Just like he did in Pueblo."

The two men's conversation really peaked my interest. "Excuse me gentlemen, my name is Logan Hayes, and I couldn't help but overhear you talking about this Bart Hickey. Would you mind telling me what happened the other night between him and those soldiers?"

Both men looked at Logan and noticed he was wearing a gun, and that it was tied down like a professional gun fighter. After looking back at each other, it was apparent neither of them wanted any trouble with this man. Emmitt took the lead. "Look here, Mr. Hayes, we don't want any trouble. If you're a friend of Bart Hickey's we'll just finish our drinks and be on our way."

"Relax gentlemen, I am not a friend of this Mr. Hickey. I don't even know him."

"Then what's your interest in him?" Warren asked.

"I am headed up to Cottonwood Pass to do some elk hunting, and I want to know who to stay clear of."

Relieved that this man wasn't an associate of Hickey's, Emmitt started telling the story. "Believe me Mr. Hayes, he's definitely one to avoid. Those two soldiers were just enjoying themselves when one of them accidentally bumped into Hickey. The soldier was trying to apologize when Hickey up and drew on him. He had reared the hammer back on his pistol and was ready to kill the soldier. He would have done it too, if it hadn't been for one of the four men riding with him saying they didn't need any trouble with the army. So Hickey shoved the soldier away from the bar and told him and his buddy to get out before he shot them both."

"You seem to know this Hickey pretty well. What else can you tell me about him?"

"He and his gang were a bunch of claim jumpers, robbing and killing miners around Pueblo back in 58' and 59'. The problem was, no one could prove anything against them. Mainly because they didn't leave any witnesses. But then they up and killed the local sheriff. The sheriff was well liked by the town's people, so they put a posse together and went after them all. Hickey and his gang hightailed it out of the area before the posse could catch and hang them."

"And you are certain that this man from the other night was Hickey?"

"Sure as my name is Emmitt. I was a member of that posse."

"It sure would help if you could give me a description of him." Logan wanted to put a face to the tracks he had been following.

Emmitt was more than willing to provide Logan with Hickey's description. "He's a big fella, I'd say he's about your height. You'll recognize him right off, he has blond hair and blue eyes. Quicker and deadlier than anyone I know of with a gun, and meaner than a snake. As far as I know there is still a wanted poster on him in Pueblo for $5,000, if you're interested. Guess he returned figuring no one would recognize him after near onto ten years."

"Emmitt, Warren, I want to thank you both for talking to me, and giving me the history on this Hickey character. Bartender, give these gentlemen two more beers each on me." With that Logan placed a silver dollar on the bar and walked out. He now had a good idea about the five men riding out ahead of him. Along with a good description of their leader Hickey.

The next morning I ate a hearty breakfast at the café. Then loaded up and continued northwest along the Arkansas River. It appears that the territory is starting to fill up with lots of bad men. Not knowing what lay ahead, and not being one to take anything for granted, I checked the loads in my weapons. Then preloaded the extra two cylinders for my Remington pistol, and placed them in the special cartridge loops on the front of my gun belt.

Around noon, with the sun high in the sky, I rode into the burnt out ruins of Bent's Old Fort. After starting a small fire and putting on a pot of coffee, I took the time to get used to the natural sounds around me. I can do without a lot, but coffee is not one of them when I'm traveling. I was staring around at the old ghost town while enjoying a cup of coffee, and chewing on a slice of jerky, when I heard a hoof strike a stone behind me. Spinning around on my heels I drew my pistol.

Walking into my camp was an old prospector leading a donkey packed down with mining supplies. "Hold on there pard, I don't mean you no harm. I didn't know you was here, or I would have helloed the camp."

Holstering his pistol Logan apologized for drawing down on the miner. "Sorry old fella, thought you might be someone else."

"Must be a might unfriendly someone else for you to draw iron on me."

"I thought you might be a man named Bart Hickey."

"You sure pick some mighty mean friends. I would be jumpy too with him dogging my trail."

"I don't know him personally. In fact I haven't ever laid eyes on him. But we are apparently traveling the same path. From the sound of it though, you seem to be pretty familiar with him?"

"What self respecting miner around these parts doesn't know about Hickey. He's been jumping claims ever since the big strike in Pueblo back in 58'. I didn't know he was back in these parts though. Where is it your headed that has put you two on the same path?"

"I am headed to Cottonwood Pass on a hunting trip. I picked up his trail back at Big Timbers and have been following it ever since."

"If you haven't seen him how do you now it's him?"

"A man by the name of Emmitt told me about him back in Las Animas."

"Emmitt would know. He was on the posse what chased Hickey out of Pueblo."

"You know Emmitt?"

"Sure, he and another man named Warren own the general store there in Las Animas. They bought it after their mine played out in Pueblo. Good men both of them. Emmitt was one of the original settlers of Pueblo, and one of only a few that remained after the big Injun raid back in 54'. He was still there when they struck gold back in 58'. Did pretty well for himself too."

Logan realized he had forgotten his manners. "My name is Logan Hayes. What is your name old timer, and where you headed that brings you to this old ghost town?"

"They call me One Nugget Charlie, on account I have only found one nugget worth anything. I had it made into a tooth, and used it to replace the one I lost in front."

Charlie opened his mouth and gave a big smile. Logan just chuckled. "Pretty fancy tooth, how about I just call you Charlie?"

"Fine with me. I'm headed up to the strike at Tin Cup, which just happens to be located in the lower part of Cottonwood Pass. I wouldn't mind a little traveling company, how about you? I know I'd enjoy listening to someone besides myself during the trek up to Tin Cup."

"Glad to have you along Charlie. I plan on skirting around Tin Cup itself, but you are welcome to tag along until then."

That night Logan enjoyed a good stew that Charlie made for supper. They talked long into the night, and after getting to know each other a little better they crawled into their blankets. The next morning they packed up and followed the Arkansas River north, which is where the mountain route of the Santa Fe Trail ended.

Chapter 5

The Federal Prison was located thirty miles from any civilization in Missouri. The three men were crouched low and the sky was dark. The weather was playing into their hands. Shortly after arriving the rain and lightning began and covered any sounds of their movements.

"Looks like it is going to be one hell'uva storm, Jasper."

"Yeah, as much as I hate riding in a storm, it will help us get away. Colton, did you bring an extra slicker for Quentin?"

"It is tied to the cantle on his saddle. Are you sure he's expecting us tonight?"

"His lawyer visited him yesterday. He told Quentin the plan and gave him the knife I gave him. He will be ready, so make sure each of you do your job."

Jasper, Colton, and Tate had ridden with Quentin Bellows for close to five years before he was arrested and sent to prison three years ago. They vowed to get him out, and it took them this long to learn about the prison and develop their plan.

At night the guard was reduced to one guard in each watch tower, and a single guard in each wing. On a dark night like tonight the watch tower guards couldn't see each other. That is why they had selected a night with a new moon, making it pitch dark. The rain and cloud cover was unsuspected, but an added condition in their favor.

Jasper had become very friendly with one of the whores in town that serviced the guards when they were in town. He made sure to treat her with respect, and always gave her an extra ten dollars every time he saw her. One of the guards she serviced happened to work in the wing Quentin Bellows was held. For fifty dollars she made a wax copy of the guard's keys, one of which opened the outside door to the wing. She was hesitant at first, not wanting to go to prison herself, but Jasper promised to take her with him when they left town. That night before riding to the prison Jasper slipped up to her room by way of the back stairs. He had no intention of taking her away, and he couldn't leave her behind to talk. When she turned her back to him to grab her bag, he cut her throat. As instructed by Jasper she had arranged for the night off and requested not to be disturbed. Her body wouldn't be found until late the next day.

Using a grappling hook, Tate threw the rope over the back wall half way between the two towers. He was experienced at doing it and it caught on the first attempt. Jasper and Colton scaled the wall and slipped over onto the catwalk. Silently they crawled to the tower closest to the wing holding Bellows. Crouched beside the tower wall they waited for the guard to walk along it and look out. When he did, Jasper sprang up and pulled the guard to him as he drove his knife into the mans throat. Quickly they jumped into the tower.

"Colton, grab his coat and hat and put them on. Wait here and walk the tower in case someone comes. You know what to do if they challenge you." Jasper went down the ladder and crossed the yard. He entered the wing Quentin was being held in using the key he had made from the wax form. The door was heavy and as he was closing it behind him it squeaked. The guard inside stood up and challenged him. "Who's there?"

Jasper cursed himself for making the mistake. Then quickly responded. "Hot coffee, I thought you could use it on such a night as this."

The guard wasn't used to receiving such a treat, but was thankful since the night had taken on a chill from the rain. "Great, I need something to warm me up."

Jasper walked forward and when he reached the guard, he pressed the barrel of his pistol into the guards neck. "Now, lets take a walk. Open that door and head to Quentin Bellows' cell. One wrong move and I'll take your head off." The prisoners watched as the two walked down the corridor. When they stopped in front of Bellows' cell, Jasper instructed him to open the cell door. It didn't take long before the other prisoners recognized it was a prison break. They were yelling to take them with them. Ignoring their pleas the three men walked back to the door leading into the wing. After entering the guards office, Bellows stabbed the guard in the back three times, severing his spine and killing him.

Outside the prison they saddled up and headed west. "Where to now Boss?"

"Kansas, Jasper."

"Kansas? Shouldn't we be headed to Mexico?"

"First we are going to kill Logan McCart for killing my brother. Then we will head to Mexico." After that they rode in silence.

The rain washed out all tracks of the men who pulled off the jail break. The only thing left behind was the rope hanging off the wall. Not knowing what direction they had went, pursuit was out of the question. So a $5,000 warrant was posted for Quentin Bellows dead or alive.

Chapter 6

Gideon had found his fortune up at Tin Cup and was headed back down to the plains. He planned on buying a small place and living his days out in comfort somewhere around Pueblo. He stopped to spend the night down inside Royal Gorge. He was washing out his eating pans and coffee pot in the river when he heard the riders coming. The gorge was narrow down in the bottom so there was no place for Gideon to run or hide. He was hopeful they would be friendly. "Evenin' gents, where y'all headed?"

Hickey looked down on Gideon from his horse and asked, "You been mining up at Tin Cup?"

Gideon didn't recognize Hickey, but from the tone in the man's voice, he knew he was in trouble. Wanting to keep his gold a secret he lied about coming from Tin Cup. "Never been there myself, I'm just here tryin' to pan a little gold out of the Arkansas river. Not havin' any luck though."

Hickey noticed the mule was loaded down, but wasn't carrying any mining tools. This meant either the old man didn't know what he was doing, or that he had already found his gold and sold all of his equipment. "I don't see a pick or shovel anywhere, not even a pan for sifting gold. What did you think, you were just going to walk into the water and pick it up with your fingers?"

"Look mister, I'm just an old man looking for some whiskey money. I don't want any trouble." Gideon thought if he could draw his gun and cover them, that they might move on. Hickey turned around to mock Gideon. As Hickey turned in his saddle Gideon drew his old Navy Colt.

One of the other four men spoke up, "Look here boss, he's got himself a big ol' gun."

The fear showed in Gideon's voice as he spoke. "Look here men, I don't want to shoot anyone. So why don't you fellers just keep on ridin'?"

"I don't think we'll ride on just yet old man. The way I figure it, you have already found your fortune. That's why you don't have any mining equipment tied atop that mule."

Gideon's hand was shaking from the fear inside him, and the weight of the navy colt in his hand was feeling mighty heavy. "Mister, I done told you. I'm just a poor old' man lookin' for whiskey money. I don't have anythin' worth takin'."

Hickey knew Gideon was lying. "That pack is awful full for someone who doesn't own anything. Cullen, get down and check those packs for gold."

Gideon couldn't wait any longer. They were going to find his gold and steal everything he had worked so hard to get. He raised his pistol a little higher, and started to cock the hammer when Hickey drew and shot. Hitting Gideon in the top of the head.

Cullen pulled out a couple of the bags stuffed in the pack and raised the pouches of gold high above his head. "There is more boss. He must have hit it big."

"Take the gold and kill the mule."

"Why don't we keep the mule boss, and let him haul our take?"

"Because someone will recognize the mule you idiot, and that will tie us to his murder. Now do what you're told." After transferring the gold to their own horses, Cullen shot the mule. Not wanting to be caught with a dead man in their camp, Hickey and his gang rode on and out of Royal Gorge.

Hickey is a dead shot, and it never entered his mind that he hadn't killed Gideon. But as Gideon was trying to pull the hammer back on his pistol, and he saw Hickey drawing to fire, his knees started to give out from under him. When Hickey shot, Gideon's legs were already buckling and he was dropping to the ground. As a result, Hickey's shot went high of its target and cut across the top of Gideon's head, instead of hitting him square in the forehead. The impact of the bullet knocked Gideon unconscious and spun him around as he fell face down facing away from Hickey. Hickey couldn't really see he had missed his target.

Four days after meeting One Nugget Charlie at the Ghost town of Old Bent's Fort, Logan and Charlie rode into Canon City. Riding up to the saloon Logan dismounted while Charlie tied up his donkey and Sallie to the hitch rail. Blue was still tied to Sallie's pack saddle.

Stepping up to the bar Logan ordered the drinks. "Bartender, we'll have a whiskey and a cold beer to chase it down."

The bartender glanced at Charlie, then looked back to Logan. He couldn't believe they were together. "Just you?"

Logan didn't appreciate the bartender's inference that they were not together. "No, give the same to my partner here, and don't give us any of that rot gut behind the bar. We want some of that good Kentucky bourbon I saw you giving those company men."

Being snide, the bartender said, "I doubt you can afford that mister."

Once again Logan was irritated by the bartender's attitude. "You let me worry about the cost, now pour."

Continuing to be rude, the bartender held out his hand. "That will be ten dollars mister, before I pour."

Logan tossed two five dollar gold pieces onto the bar. Everyone in the place noticed the gold coins, including the two salty characters standing at the end of the bar.

Canon City was established in the winter of 1858, during the Pikes Peak gold Rush, but the company jumped the claim to the town's site in 59', and built the town. Now the company runs roughshod over the independent miners and over charge them for everything.

Not much got past the attention of Charlie. And over the past few days he had learned quite a bit about Logan. But there was still a lot he didn't know. Including Logan's real name, and that he owned one of the largest ranches in the Kansas. The five dollar gold pieces tossed down on the bar for the drinks even surprised him.

Logan raised his glass of whiskey. "Here's to our partnership Charlie. You do all the work and I get all the rewards." Logan was just funning Charlie, but the two toughs at the end of the bar thought they had hit it rich up at the gold mines.

"Bartender, how much for a room tonight?"

"A room will cost you twenty dollars a piece."

"That's a little steep don't you think?"

"You want it or not?"

Money was no object for Logan, but he was choosey as to when and where he spent it. "No, I don't think we will take the room. I don't take kindly to being cheated. Therefore, I think we will just sleep under the stars again tonight."

The bartender dropped his hands below the bar's countertop. Logan had been in enough saloons to know they always kept a scattergun under the bar for trouble. "Mister, if you want to collect another dime from this place, you had better take your hands off that scattergun."

The bartender hadn't liked being called a cheat. He was sizing Logan up when Charlie spoke.

"I wouldn't try it if I was you mister. You'll be dead before that shotgun clears the top of the bar."

The bartender decided to heed Charlie's advice. After finishing their drinks Logan looked over to Charlie, "C'mon partner, let's head to the gorge and set up camp before night falls. I didn't much like that fella, I wish you hadn't warned him off."

"The deck was stacked against you Logan. After you killed him, the company would have arrested you and hung ya."

"I guess you're right. Thanks for having my back and speaking up. I don't like being taken advantage of, besides he was rude as all get out. I wouldn't have killed him, but he would not have been serving drinks for quite a while."

The two men at the end of the bar decided they would follow the tall stranger and his friend. They figured if those men could afford ten dollars for a couple drinks, then there must be a lot more money where that came from. Although the stranger appeared capable of taking care of himself, there were two of them to handle him. His side kick was just an old coot that didn't even carry a gun.

Logan looked like any other saddle tramp. After being on the trail for several days, his clothes were dirty and he didn't smell all that good either. He had wanted a room and a hot bath back at Canon City. But now he was looking forward to stopping and taking a bath in the river. It would be cold, but it was better than not taking one at all.

About half way into the gorge, they came upon the downed mule. Then they saw the body laying down by the river. "Charlie grab my extra pistol out of my saddlebags and check out the mule. Make sure he's dead. If he isn't put a bullet behind his ear."

Logan dismounted and walked over to the body. After seeing all the blood he rolled the man over with his boot. The man was unconscious and barely alive, but he was still breathing. Based on the amount of dust covering his body, he had been here in this condition for at least two days.

Charlie had just finished checking on the mule. "The mule is dead Logan, what do you want me to do now?"

"Charlie, bring me a canteen, and then scare up some driftwood for a fire."

Charlie put the pistol back in the saddlebags before grabbing the canteen and carrying it over to Logan. He looked down at the man who had been shot. "I thought I recognized that mule. This is Gideon Byrd, I have known him for some twenty years."

There was a sense of urgency in Logan's voice. "Get that firewood Charlie."

Charlie hurried away to do as Logan had asked. It was then that Logan heard the sound of horses approaching. As he remained knelt down over Gideon, he slowly slipped the leather thong off the hammer of his pistol.

The two men from the saloon rode up to see Logan bent over Gideon. "Look here Billy, they went and killed that old miner."

"That wasn't very friendly of them was it Clive."

Logan stood up and turned to face the two riders. They already had their weapons drawn, and pointed directly at him. "We found him here like this. He's not dead and we are trying to help him."

"Well that's not the story we are going to tell when we drag all your dead bodies back into town. Now why don't you make it easy on yourselves and just tell me where the rest of that gold is your holding."

Logan looked at Clive, who seemed to be in charge and giving the orders. "Mister, we don't have any gold, But if that's all you want is money, I have close to five hundred dollars in my saddlebags over there. You are welcome to it as long as you ride out of here and leave us alone."

"You think I am going to let you live after robbing you. I'd always be looking over my shoulder, just waiting for you to show up and try to kill me."

"Mister I am giving you the chance to take the money and ride out alive. Otherwise, you will force me to kill you and your partner Billy."

"Maybe you haven't noticed cowboy, but Billy and me already have our guns drawn, and your partner isn't even heeled."

"I've noticed, so I won't feel bad about killing you, knowing I didn't take advantage."

"I have had enough of your smart mouth." As Clive was pulling the hammer back to shoot, Logan drew and fired two quick shots. He had re-holstered his gun before Charlie even had time to duck. Clive and Billy were sagging in their saddles trying to figure out what just happened. They were dead before they fell out of their saddles.

Charlie walked over to the two men lying in the dirt. "They're both dead Logan. But I think you already knew that, didn't you. Where did you learn to shoot like that?"

"Charlie get the fire started and boil some water so we can clean Gideon's wound." Charlie knew not to push the issue and went on with his business. Logan removed the gear from Blue and Sallie, and used Blue to drag Gideon's dead mule outside the entrance of the gorge. This would keep the smell and flies, and any wolves it was bound to attract, away from their camp.

When Logan returned, Gideon was awake and sitting up. Charlie was busy cleaning his wound. Gideon was drinking some hot broth Charlie had made out of beef jerky. After introductions Logan asked Gideon what had happened. Gideon was still light headed, but as best he could, he told

Logan about being held up by five men, and shot by the leader.

Logan had a good idea of who they were. "Did the man who shot you have blond hair and blue eyes?"

"Sure did, howd you know that?"

"I recognized the tracks of the riders who entered the gorge leading right to you. One had a slight cut in his rear hoof, and their leader's horse has a star imprint in his horse's front shoe. Their leader is a man named Bart Hickey, who has blond hair and blue eyes."

"Those are some bad hombres. They left me for dead and stole my gold. If it weren't for you two happenin' along I would be dead."

Charlie's interest peeked after hearing about the gold. "How much gold did you have Gideon?"

"Twenty thousand. I have a mine up around Tin Cup. Figured I'd get out while the gettin' was good, and buy me a small place down near Pueblo. Figured to buy a small place and live my days out there in comfort. Guess I'll have to go back now that I'm broke again. I didn't file on the claim, but no one knows about it but me. How about you two throwin' in with me? I'll give you each an equal share."

Logan was the first to respond. "Thanks for the offer, but I am headed north to do some hunting. Charlie, what about you? It sounds like a perfect opportunity."

"I think I'll take you up on that offer Gideon. Logan, sounds like there's plenty up there for all of us. Sure wish you'd reconsider and throw in with us. We wouldn't even make you dig, all you would have to do is provide us with protection. Besides what kind of man turns down a sure thing like a proven gold mine?"

"Thanks anyway, but I will ride to the claim with you and make sure you arrive safe."

Chapter 7

Hickey and his gang rode into Salida and dismounted in front of the saloon. "Spivey, order us some drinks. I see a man over there I want to talk to, I'll be right back.

Hickey went over to the table where the man was drinking. "Hello Jack."

"Seen you come in Bart, or are you using another name now?"

"Still Bart, it's been nine years since the Pueblo incident, I don't think anyone will notice I'm back. Not if they want to stay alive anyway. This town seems pretty quiet, what happened, all the gold play out?"

"Mostly, the company out of Canon is still mining some on Pikes Peak. If I was you, I would stay clear of the company and their claims. They maintain some tough guards, and plenty of them."

"What about Tin Cup?"

"I Heard they are striking it rich up there too. Mostly individual miners right now, but there are three big outfits. The company won't move in till they clear out."

"Any law up there?"

"Not that I know of."

"Thanks Jack, I would appreciate it if you didn't mention my being back in the territory."

"I won't say anything, but if I was you I would not stick around Salida too long. Could be there are still some folks here that remember Pueblo. It might be they could recognize you."

Hickey got up and walked back to his gang at the bar. "What did you find out boss?"

Hickey was not comfortable with the idea of being recognized. "We are going to finish our beers and head out. Jack there is a friend of mine, but he says there are others around that might remember the sheriff's killing back in Pueblo."

One of the others spoke up, "C'mon boss, I was hoping to get a room and spend the night with one of these soiled doves."

"You can take orders and share in the profits, or stay here and call it quits. What will it be, you want to be rich, or have five minutes of satisfaction?"

"You know I want to be rich boss."

"Okay then, let's finish our drinks and move on." After stepping out of the saloon Hickey looked around as they were mounting up. "Marsh, I want you to hold up just south of town for three days. Take note of everyone that rides into town. I want to know if they are the law, prospectors, or just travelers. We are going to ride north along the Arkansas River. We'll camp on the second day out and wait for you."

Marsh wasn't happy being left behind. "What for boss, if they are prospectors we'll most likely see them up at Tin Cup anyway."

"I got a feeling someone has been dogging our heels ever since we left the Santa Fe Trail. And the next one of you that questions my orders is going to be dead, understand?"

In unison they all replied, "Yeah Boss."

Gideon and Charlie mounted up on the two dead men's horses. On the morning of the third day after leaving Royal Gorge, they rode into Salida.

Marsh had seen them coming and stepped back off the trail behind a stand of trees to watch them pass. He didn't recognize the two front riders, but when he saw Gideon he couldn't believe his eyes. After they were gone, he put his horse into a gallop and skirted the town, riding to catch up with Hickey.

Logan stepped up to the bar and ordered three beers. "After we finish these beers I want you two to stable the horses down at the livery. Gideon, can we purchase all the mining supplies you will need up at Tin Cup?"

"Yeah, but they charge five times what they'll cost down here."

"Alright, after stabling the horses give them all a good rub down and feed them some grain. Then meet me over at the hotel."

Charlie knew Logan liked taking care of his own horse. To have them do it was unusual. "What are you goin to do?"

"I am going to get us some rooms and shop around for information."

While Gideon and Charlie were down at the livery taking care of the horses, Logan learned Hickey and his gang had passed through two days earlier and headed north. He had no idea that one of them had been left behind to watch everyone riding into town, and to report their arrival back to Hickey.

Later they all met back at the hotel and went into the dining room. Logan ordered steak, with a side of potatoes and beans for all three of them, and paid for the meals. "Tomorrow morning I want you two to buy us another mule. Then go over to the general store and purchase any supplies you will need to start up your mine again Gideon."

Gideon looked at Logan with a sorrowful look. "Mr. Hayes, I am plum broke. I can't even afford a new shirt, let alone any new equipment."

"Don't worry about the money. I have changed my mind Gideon. I am going to stake you, and in return accept twenty percent of the claim. Since you and Charlie will be doing all the work, you both will retain forty percent each. I set up an account over at the general store earlier today. Tell him to charge my account for anything you purchase. Don't worry about the cost, just make sure you get everything you will need. Aside from the mining supplies get some extra staples for us, and extra grain for the horses."

After stocking up on supplies they saddled up and headed out of town. Just north of Salida, Logan turned due west. Gideon was confused with the change of direction. He rode up along side of Logan to find out where he was going. "Where are you takin' us, the easiest route to Tin Cup is due north along the Arkansas River. We don't usually turn west until we get well into the Sawatch Range."

"I know that, but so does Hickey. I don't want to run into him if I can avoid it. Besides, you can identify him as the man who shot and robbed you, so he can't afford to let you live. That is why we are going through Monarch Pass and then head north to Tin Cup."

"Smart thinkin', besides my claim is on the southwest side of the town. By takin' your route we can avoid goin' through Tin Cup altogether, and keep anyone from followin' us to the claim. It will be rough travelin' though."

Chapter 8

Marsh rode into camp two days later with his horse all lathered up from running. Hickey was surprised to see him riding so hard. "What's your hurry, Marsh?"

"Boss, you ain't going to believe this, but that old prospector you shot back in the gorge, he's still alive."

"That's bullshit, I shot him in the head from no more than ten feet away."

"I'm telling ya Boss, it was him, and he was riding with two other fellas."

"Law men?"

"No. One was another prospector, and the other one was a tall cowboy. He wasn't the law, but he didn't look like no prospector neither. Looked more like a gunfighter if you ask me."

Hickey didn't like the idea of the miner having hired a gunfighter. "I thought we took all that miner's money, he must have had enough on his person to hire himself some protection. Probably promised him part ownership of his mine."

Cullen expressed his concern. "What if he tells people up in Tin Cup that we shot him, and that we're headed there?"

"He doesn't even know our names, Cullen. Besides, he probably thinks we high tailed it south down to Mexico with all that gold we took from him. I am more worried about that cowboy. Why would he hook up with a couple old timers like that?" Hickey was truly bothered by the fact that there was someone who could identify him for attempted murder. "We will set up an ambush right here, and kill them when they ride through."

Hickey and his gang waited for three days, but the cowboy and two old prospectors never showed. "Let's ride boys. They aren't coming. Either they decided to quit, or they took another route. If they went another way we will find them up around Tin Cup. Maybe by then that old man will have dug out some more gold for us, and then I can kill him all over again."

Hickey and his men were leaving the western edge of the Sawatch Range, and were about three miles east of Tin Cup when they rode up on the cabin.

Two Time Benny was sitting out on his small porch. He was called "Two Time", because he had already found his fortune twice before. First at the Pueblo strike, then again outside of Canon City. But each time he lost it all gambling. Benny didn't like the looks of the men on their horses staring down at him. "Howdy fellers, what can I do ya fer?"

Hickey gave him a disgusted look, "What's your name old timer?"

"They call me Two Time Benny, how about you, what's your handle?"

"This is a nice little cabin you got yourself, how about gold, you having any luck?"

"Sorry to disappoint you mister, but I'm just a poor old miner. I haven't pulled out even a smidgen of gold from this lousy claim. The only thin' I got is this here cabin." That wasn't true, but Two Time wasn't going to sign over his claim to these owl hoots.

Hickey was quick to anger and he was getting impatient. "To answer your first question they call me Hickey, mean anything to you?"

"Seems I heard tell of you when I was down in Pueblo and Canon City. None of it any good."

"Then you know I ain't here for the conversation. If you want to live, you'll give us your gold and sign over this here claim right now, and move on."

"Look here son, this is all I got in the ways of a home. I don't intend on givin' it to the first owl hoot comes around blowin' hard."

Hickey was tired of talking so he drew and shot Two Time, taking the top of his head off. "Looks like we got us a gold mine boys, make yourselves at home. Spivey, take that old man's body out into the woods and bury him deep. I don't want any animals digging him up and someone finding him."

Knowing Hickey's temper, Marsh didn't want to challenge him, but went ahead and asked anyway. "Boss, what do we say if someone comes around asking about him?"

"Just tell them he sold out to us and headed down to the flatlands. Tomorrow we will check out his mine and see if he was lying about finding any color. In the meantime, look around the cabin and see if he has any sacks of gold hidden away. We can use this claim to satisfy any curiosity as to where we get all the gold we steal from the other mines and cash in."

Chapter 9

Logan had traveled half way through Monarch Pass when he turned due north. Travel through the pass had been more difficult than he had imagined it would be. There are no developed trails through Monarch Pass, as there are through the Sawatch Range, and Logan hadn't counted on the terrain being as rough as it was.

Charlie had developed saddle sores from not being accustomed to riding. He felt the pain with every step his horse took. "Logan, I am not sure this was such a good idea. I'm not a young man anymore, and all this riding over the mountains is taking its toll on me."

"What are you complaining about Charlie, the horse is doing all the hard work." Logan felt sorry for Charlie, but he knew taking the harder route was the right decision. "Besides, would you prefer to be lying dead back there along the Arkansas River from an ambush by Hickey and his men, or put up with a few saddle sores?"

"You're right Logan. I guess it's just in my nature to complain. If it wasn't my butt it would be my feet."

"Charlie, think of all that gold you and Gideon are going to share. That ought to keep your mind off those saddle sores."

Logan was certain they were close to their destination, but he had no idea where Gideon's mine was. "Gideon, I figure we aren't but about six miles outside of Tin Cup, why don't you take the lead and guide us up to your claim."

Gideon rode around Logan and led out as he turned to the west. "Without any difficulties we should be there by sundown. It's about four miles southwest of Tin Cup, but. I'd say it's only two miles from where we are right now."

Charlie let out a big whoop, "Yahoo, I am ready for a nice venison steak. Let's hurry up and get there."

Logan laughed, "I thought you were tired?"

"I was until I learned we would be stopping for good tonight. Now quit jawing and get moving."

As they rode up to the mine everything looked quiet, and it didn't appear anyone was around. "Gideon, why don't you look up inside the mine and make sure we are alone. Could be someone has squatted on your claim since you have been gone. Charlie, you start a fire and slap those steaks on to cook, and don't forget the coffee. I will take care of the horses and scout the perimeter for sign."

The claim was empty of any nesters. The mine was pretty much as Gideon had left it, with the exception of a small cave-in about midway back. Aside from some weathering and a couple loose boards that had fallen out of place, the sluice was still in good shape. Gideon had been very careful to never disclose the location of his mine. And not wanting to get robbed, he hadn't said anything to anyone about leaving the mountain. So it was doubtful anyone even knew he had been gone.

Logan returned to camp and knelt down to pour himself a cup of coffee. "I didn't find any tracks to indicate anyone has been around. So I think we are safe and alone for now. I will ride into Tin Cup tomorrow and see if I can pick up any information on the local conditions. Maybe someone has seen Hickey."

The next morning Charlie and Gideon began making repairs to the sluice, and clearing the cave-in to open the shaft. Logan saddled up Dusty and packed his supplies atop Sallie and Blue.

Gideon was watching Logan pack, but was curious as to why he had packed up all his belongings. He got a sinking feeling in his stomach at the thought that Logan was pulling out for good. "Are you leavin' us already? I thought you would stick around for a couple days and make sure your investment was protected."

"I'll be back. I want anyone watching me to believe I am only on a hunting trip. If I ride in on Dusty and don't have any supplies, no one will ever believe my story. By taking Sallie and Blue, there won't be any reason to question my being here for any other reason than to hunt."

Gideon's churning stomach settled down with the thought that Logan would be returning. "Always thinkin' ahead, I like that about you Logan."

As I rode down the lone street of Tin Cup, everyone in town had their eyes glued to me. Probably because I looked more like a gunfighter than a miner. They hadn't had any trouble with claim jumpers up to now, and they were very curious as to who this hombre was riding into town with no mining supplies. They had heard the stories of miners being robbed in the foothills below as they left the pass.

Just like any other newcomer I pulled up at the tent acting as a saloon. By the time I had dismounted and tied Dusty to the rail, Sallie had caught up with Blue in tow. Releasing the lead rope that was hook over her pack saddle, I tied it to my saddle horn. When I stepped inside my vision wasn't adjusted to the dark. So I stepped to the side to get accustomed to the dim light before stepping up to the bar. Looking around I didn't see anyone I knew. I was specifically looking for a man with blonde hair and blue eyes. Not seeing him, or anyone else that presented a threat, I walked up to the bar to quench my thirst. "Bartender, how about a cold beer?"

"Coming right up." The bartender wasn't any different than any other one I had ever known, and as such, he wanted to know my business. "Stranger to these parts aren't you? Come to find your fortune?"

"I have been to the Rockies on a couple occasions. But this is my first visit to Tin Cup. I am up here on a hunting trip."

By now several of the town's folk had followed me in, they were curious to learn more about me. However, they were content to let the bartender ask all the questions. "Just what are you hunting, if not gold?"

"Elk. I understand some of the biggest are located up here in Cottonwood Pass."

"You heard right. Why I have seen some that are as big as the moose out of Canada."

"Great, I hope I have the good fortune of finding a couple of them." One of the patrons who had checked my packs out before coming in spoke next. "I noticed your carrying an old Hawken. Haven't seen one of those for years. Most hunters use a Sharps rifle these days."

"It was my father's musket. I grew up hunting with it, and never saw a need to replace it with anything new."

Some of the other townsmen were moving in closer to listen to the conversation. But it was the same man who continued asking the questions. "I suppose you have heard about the gold strike up here in the Pass?"

Logan knew they were feeling him out. "Been hearing about it ever since I rode through Las Animas. But I'm sure you have already checked out my packs, and noticed I don't have any mining equipment."

"We also noticed you wear that hog leg mighty comfortable like. Wouldn't be your looking to find gold the easy way would you?"

Logan didn't like the accusation, "Mister, what is your name?"

"Dan Clady, and I am the spokesman for the town's local peace keeping committee. Now it's your turn, who might you be?"

"My name is Logan Hayes. I am not looking for trouble, but I like to be prepared for it. Seems like I have been traveling behind a group of killers ever since I left the ruins at Big Timbers. All I have been able to determine is that their leader is a man named Bart Hickey. Have you heard of him?"

"Seems there were some stories of him a ways back. But the way I heard it he left the country some nine years ago, just ahead of a hangman's noose. Ain't heard anything about him being up in this area, or any sightings of him."

"I could be wrong, but I have reason to believe he is headed this way. So if I was you I would spread the word. He has a short temper, and likes to shoot first and ask questions later."

Clady relaxed his poor attitude toward Logan. "Mr. Hayes, you look like you can handle yourself pretty good, and after talking with you, I believe you to be an honest man. We could use a good man for protection and to keep the peace. Would you consider taking on the job of town sheriff since you don't have any intentions of mining?"

"I don't have an interest in wearing a badge either." I didn't say it to Clady, but it has been my experience, that eventually the town folk would turn against the very man they hired for protection. In addition, unwilling to support him when danger threatens them. "Thanks for the offer, but I am just up here to hunt."

"We will pay you $500 a month, provide you a cabin to live in, and free meals at the local canteen."

"That is a mighty tempting offer, but I think I'll just stick to hunting elk."

I finished my beer and walked out of the saloon. Leaving the local residents buzzing about me. Not wanting to give anyone the wrong idea of where I was headed, I rode out of town to the north. About a mile out of town, and sure no one was trailing me, I turned west and circled around Tin Cup to return to Gideon's mine.

Chapter 10

Logan filled Charlie and Gideon in on his conversation with Dan Clady in the saloon. Including the offer of town sheriff and all the benefits that went with the job. "Hickey hasn't shown his face in town. But I'd bet my horse that he's in the area, and you know how much I like that horse, Charlie."

"You aren't going to take the job are you?"

"No, I have no interest in putting a target on my chest. Besides I still want to go hunting and have some alone time. How are things in the mine?"

Gideon was happy to tell him the status of the mine. He was hoping it might persuade Logan to stick around. "We opened up the shaft and started sifting. Found a few good sized nuggets already. I know there is a solid vein running through there somewhere, we just have to find it. Charlie found a spot inside the shaft where he thinks we should change direction and sink a shaft straight down."

"Let's go have a look. I want to see where you're talking about." The shaft only ran back about a hundred yards. They stopped about half way in.

"This is the spot Logan, what do you think?"

"Charlie, I think you picked the right spot, but if you look careful, the quartz vein runs up, not down. I think you would be better off going up instead of sinking a shaft down. Also, you see that rust colored rock up in the ceiling. That is another indication that the gold is above you and not down below."

Gideon was surprised by Logan's knowledge of mining. "I thought you didn't know anythin' about mining."

"I said nothing about knowing how to find it. I just said I didn't want to expend my energy digging for gold."

"Any other suggestions?" Charlie asked.

"Yes, from here on you need to shore up the walls. You can build a scaffold as you go up to make it easier to mine, and to keep it from falling in around you."

It was Charlie still asking the questions. "How do you expect two old coots like us to cut all that wood and mine at the same time. Besides we don't know the first thing about buildin' a scaffold, whatever that is."

"I will hang around for a while and cut the timber. Also, I want to lay in some logs for skids. That way the you can use your donkey and the mule we bought down in Canon City to haul out the rock and ore. Then you two will not have to work so hard getting it down to the sluice."

Gideon was feeling guilty. "Logan, you should have an equal share along with me and Charlie. You staked this outfit, and now you are puttin' in way more work than you originally intended. Not to mention the fact that we couldn't do it ourselves."

"Thanks Gideon, but twenty percent will be just fine. Besides, if I am right about that vein being above us, we will all have more money than we could ever hope to spend."

The first thing Logan built was a sled. Then he made a harness out of some young saplings and rope for Gideon's mule to pull the sled. The saplings provided more give than the harder tree limbs.

I could hear Gideon yelling at his mule while I was cutting timber. "You stubborn hammer head, get up there."

It was Charlie that suggested the name. "You should name him Thor, after that Greek god that swings that hammer."

"Good idea Charlie, it's shorter than hammer head. Besides, he might think I'm talkin' to you when I yell out hammer head." Everyone laughed.

I spent the next few days felling trees for skids and shoring planks. I made a point of not using any trees close to the mine, and didn't take too many from any one spot. This would help protect the location of the mine, and keep any passers by from being to inquisitive.

Thor did more than his share of work, and he proved to be tireless. Gideon and Charlie split the logs I cut. After a week we had the rails set into the mine and down to the sluice, along with enough planks to shore up the mine shaft where they would be working. I supervised the work inside the mine, and showed them the proper way to shore up the walls and build the scaffold with a walkway.

It's been three weeks since they have been preparing the mine to make it safe enough to start the new shaft upward. "I think you two are ready to start mining that gold now. Just keep shoring up the walls and walkway as you go. Do it just like I have showed you, and it will remain strong enough to hold your weight. I am leaving tomorrow to head up into the pass and do some hunting."

Charlie was deeply saddened at Logan's announcement, and it showed in his voice as he talked. "We are going to miss you Logan. But I wish you luck on your hunt. We will wait right here until you get back. How long do you think you'll be gone?"

"I should be back in about six weeks. First, I want to scout the country to get a better feel and knowledge of the countryside before I do any actual hunting. Then I plan on taking the meat to the Arapaho camp over to the northeast along the Arkansas River. If any Arapaho or Cheyenne show up, just mention you are friends of mine, and that I am part owner of the mine. I am blood brother to both tribes, so you will not be harmed. Charlie, I will be taking Blue and Sallie. I want you to take good care of Dusty for me while I am gone."

"Don't worry, I'll treat her just like she was my very own child. But why take Blue instead of Dusty?"

"Because Blue blends into the background better."

Chapter 11

"Marsh, you take Dillon and Porter, and go into Tin Cup. I want you to scout the outskirts of town and get a good look at the independent miners and their operations. Then go into town and see what kind of law they have. Make sure you avoid trouble, so don't rob or shoot anyone. In fact, before you ride into town, put your pistols and gun belts in your saddlebags. If anyone asks about your business, tell them you bought this place from Benny, and that you are working the mine."

"What if they ask about Benny?"

"Just tell them he went down off the mountain. Said something about goin to Sante Fe. It is far enough away that no one should try to verify his location."

After scouting the mining camps close to town, the three men rode into Tin Cup. It wasn't long after they entered the saloon, that Clady came up to them at the bar. "Howdy gents, how are you doing?"

Marsh did the speaking, "Fine, thought we would stop in and wash some of the dust out of our throats."

"I haven't seen you three around here before. Do you plan on doing some mining?"

"Sure do. Fact is we just bought a claim northeast of town."

"Really, I didn't know there were any mines for sale. Which mine did you purchase?"

"Two Time Benny's."

"That's very surprising, I didn't know he was looking to sell. It's also unusual that he would have left without mentioning it, or saying goodbye before leaving."

Dillon snapped back, "What's it to you mister, are you the land agent around here or something?"

Marsh kicked Dillon in the shin. "Don't pay any attention to him mister. He's still a little cranky from the long ride up from Santa Fe. We were cutting wild longhorns out of the breaks to sell when we heard about the gold strike, and thought we would give it a try. Sounded easier than rounding up a bunch of ornery steers and having to herd them to market through Indian territory. Benny said his mine was all played out, and that he was too tired to keep mining. So he sold it to us cheap. Without any equipment we thought we would be better off buying an ongoing mine than to try starting from scratch."

"Can't blame you there, but I thought Two Time had found a good strike."

"Well, whatever his reasons, he sold us the mine and we plan on trying to find our own fortune."

"I wish you luck, if you have any questions about mining, folks around here will be more than willing to help."

"Thanks, although, we are a little concerned about claim jumpers. Do you have any law around here to keep the peace?"

"Not specifically, some of us town folk make up a committee to keep the peace. We offered a gentleman the job of sheriff just yesterday, but he declined."

"What, was he scared or something?"

"I doubt it. He looked like he could handle himself pretty good. Said he was going hunting for elk up north. Big fella, riding a dun horse. Maybe you seen him on your ride in from your claim."

"Can't say that we did. I guess we'll just finish our beers and get back to our mine. Thanks for the information."

"You're welcome, and don't be strangers, come back and visit us sometime. You know what they say about all work and no play."

Clady walked off and the three men went back to drinking their beers. Dillon's shin was still hurting, and he was mad at Marsh. "Why did you kick me?"

"Bart said he didn't want any trouble, and we needed to get some information out of that man. Not chase him away and make him suspicious."

"A lot of good that did, we didn't learn a thing from him."

"Sure we did. We know there isn't any law in town. We also know that big man I saw riding with the miner boss shot back in the gorge is here. Which means those two miners are here too."

"How do you know that?"

"Because he said the man he offered the sheriff's job was riding a big dun. That's the same horse I saw him riding back in Salida."

After a couple more beers they returned to the mine. Hickey was glad to hear the information. "Good job Marsh. Now I want the four of you to go work the mine a bit. I don't care if you find anything, I just want it to look active. Tomorrow we will ride out and find some gold the easy way."

The next morning Hickey was ready to ride when Marsh approached him. "Boss, that Clady fella seemed to think Two Time had struck gold, maybe we should look around some more and work the mine for real."

"That sounds okay to me Marsh. In fact why don't you and Spivey stay back and work the mine. The rest of us will take care of what needs done today. That way, if anyone comes snooping around, it will make our cover story look all that much better.

Jeb and Arlo were busy panning for gold when they heard the riders coming. They were finding a few nuggets and some dust above the rip rap in the stream. "Jeb, sounds like we got company."

"Let's quit for the day Arlo. We aren't having any luck anyway. We can offer them some venison stew for a little conversation."

Hickey and his gang rode up and waited for Jeb and Arlo to step out of the stream. Hickey did the talking as always. "Having any luck boy's?"

"No, the only thing we have for our hard work today is cold feet. Why don't you gent's light a shuck and join us for a bowl of stew?"

"Mighty small camp you have here, are you sure you have enough?"

"It's the only thing we do have. I don't think we have pulled more than a couple hundred dollars out of here all total."

"I think we'll take you up on that stew. We are new to these parts, maybe you can tell us where we might set up our claim without intruding on the other mines."

While they ate, Jeb filled Hickey in on the more prosperous miners and their locations. "So you can see, most all of the best places around town have been claimed. The only place I don't know about is southwest of here. As far as I know that's pretty open country. But it seems like if there was any gold over there, someone would have found it by now. You might try farther north higher up in the pass."

These two men didn't have enough gold for Hickey to bother stealing. But he didn't want them telling anyone else about him asking so many questions about the other mining operations. "Cullen, Porter, grab these two and hold them."

Jeb and Arlo were confused about what was happening. "Hold on there partner, we done told you we don't have any gold worth taking."

"I don't want your gold old fella, but I can't have you yapping to anyone that you saw us. Dillon, shoot them with their own guns. I want it to look like they killed each other."

Dillon collected their pistols and shot each one in the chest with the other's gun. Then he placed them face down facing each other, and then placed their pistols in their hands. After a quick search Hickey found their small pouch of nuggets and placed it in Jeb's empty hand.

Porter didn't understand why they weren't keeping the gold. "Boss, why do that?"

"I want the town's folk to believe the two fought over their own gold. If we take it they will figure it for a robbery. The information we got from them is far more valuable than that little pouch of gold."

The killings of Jeb and Arlo were the talk of Tin Cup the next day. Word spread quickly throughout the mining community. Some folks didn't believe Jeb and Arlo would kill each other, no matter what it looked like. But most knew how gold fever affected even the best of men. They wrote it off to just another falling out between partners arguing over who owned what share of the gold. Besides the gold hadn't been taken. Meaning it couldn't have been a robbery.

Based on the information he got from Jeb and Arlo, there was no use to ride over to the southwest. They would jump the independent claims first, and hit the big outfits last.

For the next two weeks Hickey and his gang jumped the smaller claims. Forcing the men to sign over their claims before killing them and stealing their gold. They always buried the men to avoid too many questions, and then resold the claims to newcomers.

Marsh was in town when he heard the news that someone coming in from the west had stopped by a couple old men mining about four miles southwest of town. From the description given, he knew it was Gideon and the other miner he had seen him with in Salida. He immediately reported this to Hickey. "What are we going to do Boss? If they come to town they will tell Clady all about us."

"Looks like we will have to step up our plans. But before we can hit the bigger claims we'll have to take care of that big man that's hunting up north. We can take care of the other two on our way west to California. Besides, they will be sure to have taken a lot more gold out of that old codger's mine by then."

"Boss, between our own diggings and the other robberies we have about sixty thousand dollars. Why don't we clear out while we can?"

"Because we can more than triple that. We can quit for good with two hundred thousand. That's forty thousand apiece. Then we can split up and live in peace as rich men." It was too early to say anything now, but Hickey had no intention of sharing equally, it has always been his intent to keep the lion's share of the money.

"Marsh, you and Spivey continue to work the mine. Keep your ears open for any trouble coming out of Tin Cup. I will take the other boy's with me to track down this hunter. It's obvious he helped that miner I shot in the gorge, so it stands to reason he knows about us. We have no choice but to kill him to keep him from talking."

Chapter 12

Having spent the last two weeks riding the northern range of the Pass, I have come to enjoy its peacefulness, and shed what grief remained of my parents death. After familiarizing myself with the lay of the land I made a trip over to the Arapaho camp, which was just to the east along the Arkansas River. It was important that I visit and let them know I would be hunting in the area. Their food supplies were very low, so I promised to return with the meat from my hunt.

Returning to the Pass from my visit to the Arapaho, I found a natural cave that was big enough for me and my horses. It was perfect for using as a base camp during my hunt. Inside the cave was a natural spring, and there was an open chimney in the back. I would have plenty of water, and the chimney had enough of a draft that it took the smoke from my fire right out the top.

As far as I knew, I was the only one in the area. I had no reason to expect otherwise, and had no idea that I was being stalked by Bellows and his men. Since leaving Tin Cup I hadn't given Hickey a second thought. Today was the first day of actual hunting, I brought Sallie along to haul the carcass back to the cave. Aside from the fact that she was more suited to traveling the rough terrain than Blue. It was a tremendous advantage not having to maintain a hold on her lead rope. And although Blue was very strong and a good roping horse, Sallie was less disturbed by the smell of blood.

I had been tracking a large elk and traveled three ridges over from the cave when I caught sight of him. He was moving slowly as he fed along the top of the next ridge over. I was some what amazed, and thought to myself. *"I'll be damned, it is as big as one of those Canadian moose."* I moved down into the bottom of the ravine, so as not to spook him, or give him my scent. Then I quickened my pace to get in front of the elk. What I didn't know was that Hickey and his men were tracking me from atop the ridge to my back at the same time.

It was just luck that Hickey was able to find McCart. They didn't know about his cave, or that the mule was trailing behind another ridge over. They too had been watching the big elk feed when they heard Logan disturb some loose leaves in the ravine below. Staying far enough back from the ridge and out of sight, they followed Logan while he continued to close in on the elk.

Logan didn't know if it was the Indian spirits or what, but for some reason he got the feeling he wasn't alone atop this mountain. Stopping, he looked back over his shoulder. He scanned the ridge floor and the ridge behind him, but didn't see or hear anything else. Logan discounted the feeling of being followed to Sallie trailing him.

Hickey got concerned when Logan stopped and looked back in their direction. It could have been because he heard them, but when Logan continued on as if nothing was wrong, he knew that they had not been detected. "Boy's, dismount and tie up your horses. Porter, grab your Sharps. We will follow him on foot from here. Be careful where you walk. We don't want him to know we're following him."

Dillon had the least patience of the three. "Boss, he is only one man carrying a single shot musket and a pistol, why don't we just rush him. He would be dead before he even knew what happened."

"No, if we failed he would vanish into the woods. Then we would play hell catching him unaware again. He strikes me as a man who can take care of himself in the woods. Porter, I want you to get up ahead of us. If I am right, it looks like that ravine plays out up ahead, and then he will be forced to go up the other side. Take the shot the first good chance you get. You will only get one chance so make it count."

"You got it Boss." Porter picked up his pace and beat everyone, including Logan, to the edge of the cliff at the end of the ravine. Picking a spot that gave him a clear view of the hill on the other side of the ridge, he laid down and sighted in his Sharps. He estimated the distance to be about three hundred and fifty yards. He was usually right, having been a sharpshooter in the southern army, and killed many men in the same manner during the war.

Looking down, Logan had stopped to get a closer look at the track he saw. The elk had apparently come down from the top and crossed over the side of the mountain. Looking around he couldn't see it anywhere. It could be an old track, and not seeing the big animal, Logan wanted to make sure the track was fresh. He bent over to get a closer look. That simple move saved his life. For just as he bent over Porter took his shot. Instead of hitting Logan square in the back of the head, the bullet cut a deep gouge that ran from his neck to the top of his head. Between bending over and the force of the bullet, Logan fell over the side of the mountain. It was only luck that his reflexes caused him to tighten his grip around the Hawken. The strike of the bullet had knocked him out instantly.

They all saw him fall over the side of the mountain. Porter let out a Rebel yell, "Wa-woo, Boss, I got him."

"Dillon, get down there and make sure he is dead."

The steepness of the ridge didn't allow for good footing. Dillon mostly slid down into the bottom of the ravine. Looking over the edge of the mountain, he could tell the trek down to McCart would be much more difficult than having slid down the ridge. "I see him boss, he isn't moving and looks to be dead. His head and face are all bloodied. Hell, if the shot didn't kill him, the fall most certainly had to finish him. It's too steep to get down to him."

"Alright, come on back and let's get out of here in case someone heard the shot."

Hickey and his gang were sure Logan was dead, and rode away. "Now we can hit those big claims without any interference. When we're finished we'll take care of those two old timers."

Once again Hickey's gang made the mistake of not verifying their work was complete, and making sure Logan was dead. He was unconscious, and because of all the blood, it appeared to Dillon that his head had been blown apart. It would have taken some effort, but Dillon could have gotten down to check, he was just too lazy. Hickey took his word for it when he said it was too steep.

Chapter 13

The night passed and a heavy dew fell. When Logan woke up it was morning, he was soaking wet and chilled to the bone. Between the wetness and loss of blood, his body temperature had dropped. Not sure of the time he laid there shivering. He realized that his clothes were all wet, and that he had been there all night if not longer.

The last thing Logan remembered was looking at a fresh track. He tried to move and sit up but couldn't. Then he wiped the moisture off his face, thinking it was water from the dew, to his surprise it was blood.

Loosening the grip on my musket I reached up to feel the back of my head that was throbbing with pain. I could feel the deep furrow running the length of the back of my head. It was to narrow and straight to have happened from the fall. Rocks and trees would not have made such a clean cut. The only other explanation was that I had been shot. As far as I could tell, the bullet only went scalp deep and didn't penetrate the skull. I was drenched in my own blood, and my mouth was bone dry. It felt as if someone had poured a bucket of sand into my mouth. Stretching out my arm, I reached out and pulled a low hanging tree limb to me, and sucked the water off the leaves. Feeling nauseous, and with my whole body racked with pain, I started checking out the rest of my body as best I could. Wiping the blood off my face I felt several lacerations, most likely caused by the fall. Feeling my sides it felt like I had a couple broken ribs. But I still didn't know why I was unable to move anything but my head and arms. It was apparent that one of my ankles was very swollen by the way it pushed against my moccasin. And although I couldn't see any broken bones sticking out of my legs, I couldn't be sure they weren't broken. Especially since I couldn't move to reach them. Straining my neck I could see where my jeans had been ripped, and that there was a large gash oozing blood just above my right knee. I slipped my right arm behind my back to feel around. There didn't appear to be any serious break in my back, but I could have hurt my spine and just not been able to feel the damage with my hands.

At this point I could only hope the strike of the bullet has somehow temporarily paralyzed me from the waist down. Unfortunately, being paralyzed is just as bad as having a broken back, because I'm still unable to defend myself. At some point, while I was taking stock of my wounds and considering the spot I was in, I passed out.

It wasn't until the next morning that I woke up. I was in serious trouble, somehow I had to get back to the cave, but it wasn't long before I passed out again.

The next time Logan woke up he started vomiting uncontrollably. Based on the light filtering through the trees, it was around four in the afternoon. It hadn't occurred to him to check for his weapons before, sliding his arm down his side, he placed his hand down over his gun belt.

His pistol is missing. It must have fallen out when he tumbled down the cliff.

I'm in no shape, or willing to expend what little energy I have to try and find my pistol. My knife is still in its sheath, and I still have my Hawken musket. Unfortunately, all my extra powder and shot is in my pack aboard Sallie. Assuming the powder in my Hawken is still dry, I will only have one shot for protection.

One thing is for certain, if I stay here I will die for sure. Somehow I will have to drag myself back to the cave before the wolves find me. Which won't be long with all the blood I have spilled. I'm surprised they haven't already gathered for the kill from the scent. The cave is less than a day's walk, but with my injuries I'm thinking it will take me three or four days at best to drag myself back. I don't know what would be worse, the wolves eating me, or dying from starvation and thirst. Using my hands I pushed myself up onto my side, and rolled over onto my belly. Slipping my Hawken over my neck, I reached out with my arms and started dragging myself back up the mountain. With any luck I could reach the floor of the ravine before dark.

It was slow going, and I had been dragging myself up the steep cliff for about three hours, when I saw the edge of the ravine just above me. My hands are raw from gripping the rocks and trees to pull myself up, and I have left a trail of blood for any predators to follow. The pain throughout my whole body has increased, and my strength is all but gone from the effort. The only solace I can take from the pain, is that it's a good sign my spine isn't broken. The fact that I can feel pain gives me hope that I was right, and that the paralysis may only be temporary.

As tired as I am, I know I can't stay on the side of this cliff. After stopping for a short rest, I started once more to heave myself up the mountain. It was then that I heard a horse moving up above. I began to think they might have left one man behind to make sure I was dead. I quit dragging myself and slid the Hawken off my neck. I'm thankful I still have the use of my arms and hands, and can still move my head. Laying very still, I aimed my rifle toward the top of the ledge. I was going to shoot whoever poked their head over the side. I pulled up the slack on the trigger, and was just about to fire when Sallie poked her head over the ledge. Letting the tension flow from my body I softly spoke to the mule. Trying to make it easier, I slipped the Hawken around a tree, and used it for leverage to pull myself to the top of the cliff. After repeating this process about five more times, I reached the top of the cliff and dragged myself onto the floor of the ravine.

It will be dark in an hour or so and I have to prepare for the night. Even though I am feeling very sick and weak, I have to get my supplies off Sallie before passing out again. Sliding underneath her belly I took out my knife. If I accidentally slip and cut her, she will most likely kick me to death. So as carefully as I could, I cut the cinch on the sawbuck pack saddle and watched it fall to the ground. The first thing I reached for was my canteen. After washing my mouth out to clear the taste of the vomit, I took a long hard drink. Between the loss of blood, vomiting, and lack of water, I was seriously dehydrated. Next I rummaged around to find the jerky and a box of matches. While chewing on a stick of jerky I gathered some sticks close by and got a small fire started. Aside from the warmth, that I so desperately needed, it might help keep the wolves away. I would have to rely on Sallie to protect me from the wolves if I pass out again. Shortly thereafter Logan lost consciousness. By the time he came to, the sun was already high in the sky.

I am not strong enough to drag myself all the way back to the cave, and I can't get up on Sallie. A smile came across my face as I thought to myself. *"When this is over I am going to have to teach Sallie how to lay down on command."* It was as I was humoring myself, and staring at the supplies on the pack saddle that the idea came to me. I grabbed the rope I was going to use to tie down the dead elk onto the pack saddle. Then maneuvering the pack saddle sideways and pushing it behind Sallie, I strung the rope through it. After tying off one end of the rope to the saddle, I crawled forward under Sallie's neck. It took me six tries, but I was able to toss the rope high enough and over her neck. Then I repeated the process a second time so the rope would not slip off while dragging me.

Taking hold of the loose end of the rope, I drug myself back to the pack saddle and tied off the rope to the other side of the saddle. Closing the pack, I pushed it up onto the pack saddle, then crawled on top. With my chest lying on top of the pack, I gripped the rope on each side of the saddle. Using the ropes like reigns I coaxed Sallie to move out in the direction of the cave. The going was slow and rough. I had to stop often, sometimes to rest my hands, and sometimes to move rocks and logs out of my path. I had to guide Sallie around the logs and rocks too big to move with just my arms. Several times along the journey I lost consciousness. Whenever my hands released the ropes Sallie would stop.

As best as Logan could figure, it had been five days since he was ambushed. Having drank all his water he was still dehydrated. Between the dehydration, lack of food, and pain, Logan had become delirious. The only good thing was that the blood had clotted around his head and knee, stopping any further loss of blood.

I can't recall how many times I lost consciousness, but this time when I came to I could see the mouth of the cave. Before continuing on I guided Sallie to the north side of a stand of Aspens. There I gathered some moss at the base of the trees and stuffed it under my shirt. Spurred on by the encouragement of seeing the cave, I urged Sallie to step up her pace. Probably not the best idea since I bounced all over my pack, and the pain increased two-fold. The pain was almost unbearable, but I had to reach the cave.

Logan estimated it took another hour before Sallie walked into the cave. She went straight back to the spring to drink. Rolling off the saddle I dragged myself up beside her, and took a long slow drink as I listened to her fill her own belly from three days of thirst. I don't know how either of us made it without water. After drinking my fill and washing off my face, I turned my focus back to my situation. There was no getting around it, if I stayed here and didn't find help, I would die.

I slithered over to Blue and cut the hobbles off his legs so he could leave the cave and feed on the grass. I couldn't worry about him wandering off. Fact is, I couldn't take care of him in my condition. Sallie would remain close to the cave, so the best I can hope for is that Blue has bonded enough with her to stay close. It helped that the spring was inside the cave and they were not likely to stray to far from water.

Because I had planned to be in the area for at least a week, I had staged some firewood inside the cave before leaving to hunt. Using some dried grass and twigs I got a fire started, and after setting on a couple good sized logs it was roaring. Grabbing the coffee pot from along the wall of the cave, I filled it with water and placed it on the fire to boil. Then I returned to the spring to drink again. This time I drank until I couldn't drink anymore.

Taking off my neckerchief, I soaked it in the hot water to wash out the bullet crease on the back of my head. Then as best I could, I reached down and cleaned the gash above my knee.

Unfortunately I left the pot on the fire while cleaning my wounds, and now it was too hot to put my hands in. While letting it cool down I took my knife out and started cutting up my shirt. It was pretty much in shreds anyway. I cut long strips out of the sleeves to use as wraps for tying around my head and knee. Taking a large flat piece cut from the back of the shirt, I placed the moss on it and poured hot water over it to soak. Then once again cleaned my wounds with hot water. After cleaning the wounds as best I could, I cut a couple more squares out of the shirt front to hold the moss against the wounds. Then strapped them in place with the strips cut from my shirt sleeves. I learned how to use the moss packs to fight infection from the Indians.

Exhausted, I laid back to rest. When I woke up it was morning and my condition hasn't improved. I'm still unable to move from the waist down. Although I have plenty of water with the spring, I am out of food. After drinking my fill and refilling the pot, I boiled the water while removing the dressings to check my wounds. The blood has clotted again, but the moss packs are soaked with blood and used up. I didn't want to remove the scabs and start the bleeding again, so I didn't clean the wounds with water. I placed new moss packs on the scabs and tied them in place.

For the next two days Logan slipped in and out of consciousness. Mostly the result of a concussion, but partly the result of being extremely weak from the loss of blood and lack of food.

The pot still had water in it so I used the last of my coffee grounds. I could see where Blue and Sallie had been in and out of the cave to drink, so I knew they were still close. I couldn't wait any longer, I had to catch Sallie the next time she came in, and leave to get help. Logan passed out again while waiting for Sallie to return for water.

When Logan woke up the next day, he found he could sit up, but still unable to use his legs. Even so, his spirits were raised with the thought he could move around better. At a minimum, it would improve his ability to travel.

Now I know what it must be like to get kicked in the head by a horse. Dragging myself outside, I found a couple small up rooted trees and made a travois out of the canvas that made up my packs. The rope I used to drag myself back to the cave was still hanging around Sallie's neck. This made it easy to catch her up. After releasing the sawbuck saddle still dragging behind her, I tied the rope to my newly made travois. Crawling back into the cave, I gathered up my rifle and saddle holster with the pouch of extra powder and shot. Then I pulled out the extra revolver from my saddlebags. After replacing the loads I slipped it into my holster. At the very least, I now had some protection against the wolves. More importantly, protection against those who tried to kill me. Food would still be hard to kill, if at all.

Placing my saddle blanket on the travois for a pillow, I rolled over onto the travois, and laid my musket by my side. Grabbing the ropes I steered Sallie toward the Arapaho camp, thankfully Blue followed.

The going was slow so it gave me plenty of time to think about who would want me dead. The only name that came to mind was Hickey. Somehow he must have learned about my relationship with Gideon.

Chapter 14

Gideon and Charlie had been working day and night. They used the large rocks taken from the mine to build a protective wall. The wall was made into a half circle that enclosed and protected the mouth of the mine. Logan had suggested building the wall before leaving. He couldn't be sure, but was confident Hickey and his men would probably show up one day. They used full logs, cut in half, to make a gate that closed and locked over the skids. The wall stands about five feet high and provides both concealment and protection. It was about two hundred yards down to the sluice on the Taylor River.

They had found the main vein of gold. At first they couldn't believe what they were seeing. The vein was a good eight inches wide, and it was the finest quality either Gideon or Charlie had ever seen. They were pulling out about ten thousand dollars of gold a day. It had been a little over a month since Logan had left, and they were running low on staples. They decided that Charlie should take Thor and go into Tin Cup to replenish their supplies. Gideon was well known and they didn't want anyone following him back to the mine. Logan had given Charlie enough cash to purchase whatever they needed so they wouldn't have to flash gold around. Using gold to purchase supplies would put the whole area on notice, and give people the idea they had struck it rich. Not something you wanted to telegraph.

Charlie walked into town with Thor trailing behind him. The townspeople were all a buzz about something, but he couldn't make out what they were saying. The idea was to get the supplies and leave without being noticed as much as possible. As much as Charlie wanted to know what they were talking about, he didn't want to bring any attention to himself. So he went about his business without interrupting them.

As usual Clady had watched the stranger come into town, and kept an eye on him as he headed to the general store. Charlie didn't present any threat, but Clady still wanted to speak with him, to learn a little something more about him. More specifically, he wanted to find out if Charlie knew of any other strangers in the area. Especially since he had entered town from the southwest, which was unusual for any newcomer. "Howdy stranger."

Charlie turned to see Clady walking towards him. "Howdy, town seems to be all a buzz, what's going on?"

"Been some trouble as of late."

"Killings?"

"A couple, and we suspect there has been some claim jumping taking place. But we don't have any evidence."

"What makes you think it's happening if you don't have any proof?"

"There has been a lot of independent claims sold. But none of the miners have ever been seen after selling out."

"What do the new owners say?"

"That is the strange thing about it, seems they all bought theirs claims from the same man. That's what makes it so suspicious."

"You can't possibly believe I had anything do to with any claim jumping? I'm lucky enough to be holding my own body up on these old tired legs, let alone hold up a mine?"

Clady recognized the humor and laughed. "You don't strike me as someone who would stray on the wrong side of the road. Anyway, we have a description of the man selling the claims. He is a big man that stands a couple inches over six feet, with blonde hair and blue eyes. But the only ones that have actually seen him are the men who purchased the claims. I noticed you came in from the southwest, and I thought maybe you might have seen someone fitting that description?"

"No sir, I haven't, but that fits the description of a claim jumper I heard of a while back. If I'm not mistaken, he goes by the name of Bart Hickey. If it is him, y'all have big trouble on your hands."

Clady now had a name to put to the description. He was hoping the old timer could provide some more information regarding Hickey. He continued the conversation. "What is your handle?"

"They call me One Nugget Charlie." Charlie pointed to his single gold tooth.

Clady laughed again. "One Nugget, how would you like to join me for a meal, I'm buying? Your mule will be alright here outside the general store."

"I'd be pleased to, I haven't had a good home cooked meal since I left the flat lands."

"Well, I can't promise you anything other than venison. But it includes potatoes and vegetables, will that do?"

"That will do just fine."

They walked over to the tent with the wood front and a sign that read, "Mable's Café". After sitting down at a table, a large woman walked over and greeted them. "Good afternoon, how can I help you and your friend, Clady?"

"Mable, this is One Nugget Charlie, he just arrived in town."

"Pleased to meet you Charlie."

"Likewise Ma'am, it's always a pleasure to meet a handsome woman."

Mabel blushed. "Please, just call me Mabel."

"Alright Mabel, Clady say's you serve up a mean venison steak."

"I do, two venison steaks with mashed potatoes and corn coming right up. I'll bring you some coffee while you wait." With that Mabel walked away.

"Charlie, we don't get many visitors from the southwest, where is it your coming from?"

Charlie was instantly put on guard, he didn't want to provide any information that could be tied back to the mine. "I came over the Rockies from Californy. I tried my luck at the gold strike over there, but didn't have any luck. Heard they were taking it out by the buckets up here, so here I am."

"Well, that may be stretching it a little. But folks are doing pretty well. I am more interested about this fellow named Hickey. Can you tell me any more about him?"

Charlie didn't know how much they knew about Gideon, and felt it wasn't safe to mention his run in with Hickey. But still thought it was important that the town know about Hickey. "Never met the man myself. Seems some fella from Kansas on a hunting trip crossed trails with him on his way here."

Clady figured this was the same man he had offered the job of sheriff. "This hunter, did he tell you about Hickey?"

"No, I never met him either. I crossed path's with another miner that was headed to Californy. He said he had thought about coming to Tin Cup, until he met this man from Kansas. Seems the two met down in Monarch Pass. The hunter told him Hickey might be headed this way and to be careful. Turns out this miner knew Hickey from some killings and claim jumping that took place around Pueblo, back in the late 50's." Of course

Charlie was speaking from his own knowledge. "He gave me a description of the sidewinder. After that he said Californy sounded a whole lot safer than Tin Cup, and we parted ways."

Mabel brought them their steak dinners. "Here you go boys, if you need anything else just yell."

Charlie thanked Mabel and returned his attention to Clady. "How about you Marshal, you goin out looking for this Hickey fella?"

"My name is Dan Clady, Charlie, and I'm not the Marshal. But I am a member of the town's peace committee. Actually, I met this hunter you mentioned a couple months ago. I offered him the job of town Sheriff, but he politely declined and I haven't seen him since."

After finishing their meals, both men got up and walked outside. "Charlie, keep an eye out for this Hickey fellow. If you see or hear anything about him, I'd appreciate it if you were to get word back to me. Should you happen to run across this hunter, his name is Logan Hayes, let him know the offer for town sheriff still stands."

"Sure thing Mr. Clady." Charlie was not happy to hear Hickey was in the area and back to his old ways of claim jumping. After filling his list of supplies, he packed up and headed out of town. Using the same trick Logan had used, he left going north, then circled back outside of town and headed back to the mine unnoticed.

When Charlie got back he told Gideon of his conversation with Clady. Now that they knew for sure Hickey was in the Tin Cup area, they decided to strike the tent and move all their supplies up into the mine. For protection they would stay up inside the mine from here on. They couldn't protect themselves out in the open, but were pretty sure they could hold off any attack from inside the mine. Aside from their own muzzle loaders, Logan had left his Henry repeater along with 200 rounds.

Chapter 15

Clady was familiar with the old stories of claim jumping around Pueblo back in 58' and 59', but he hadn't known Hickey was the man responsible. He could not be sure whether Hickey was in the area, or that he was responsible for the missing miners. Based on the description he had, and his conversation with One Nugget Charlie, he was pretty certain it was Hickey selling the mines. Clady thought it wouldn't hurt to ride out and have a talk with this Marsh fellow that claimed to have bought Two Time Benny's mine.

Not liking the idea of going out there alone, Clady enlisted Emmitt and Flint, two other members of the town's peace keeping committee, to ride out with him.

Two Time Benny's mine was the farthest east from town. So on the way out they visited with a couple other independent miners that had recently purchased their mines. He wanted to know who it was that sold them their claims. They both confirmed having purchased their claims from a big man with blond hair and blue eyes. They really didn't much care for his looks or attitude, but since he had signed bill of sales from the original owners, there was no reason to question him. And he hadn't returned to cause them any trouble.

The three men rode up and hailed the cabin. Hickey didn't know them, and he didn't want to reveal himself. "Marsh, get out there and talk to them. Keep them talking while Spivey and Dillon get up to the mine. Spivey you and Dillon slip out the back window. Get up to the mine and dirty yourselves up like you've been working for a while."

Marsh stepped out of the cabin. "Mr. Clady, what brings you and your friends all the way out here?"

Clady took the lead. "Good afternoon Marsh, this here is Emmitt and Flint, members of the town's peace keeping committee. We have heard of some trouble with possible claim jumpers. Thought maybe you could answer some questions for us, and show us your diggings."

"You aren't accusing us of claim jumping are you Mr. Clady?"

"We don't have any proof against anyone in particular. We are just visiting the mines to put everyone on notice, and asking questions to help prevent any further trouble."

"Well, it's like I told you in town, we bought this place off Two Time Benny."

"Can you describe Benny to us?"

"Sure, he was about five foot eight, had brown scraggly hair and walked with a limp. Had something wrong with his left leg."

Emmitt turned in his saddle toward Clady. "That sounds like Benny alright."

Clady was a little relieved not to hear Marsh describe Hickey. "Sure does. Marsh, would you mind showing us your mine?"

"Well, I don't know Clady, we would like to keep it kind of private. You can understand that can't you?"

"You can trust us to keep your claim private. We are business men and have no interest in jumping your claim. Besides, everyone in the Pass already knows this mines location."

"Well, if I can't trust the citizens' peace committee, then who can I trust? Step down off your horses and follow me."

Porter was outwardly worried. "Boss, I was in town with Marsh and Dillon when we met Clady. They won't know Spivey up at the mine."

"It will be alright. They haven't seen me, and I am sure if they have any descriptions it will be mine since I sold those claims. Killing them would bring the whole town down on us. We don't want another lynch mob after us like back in Pueblo. Besides, Marsh has a good head on his shoulders, he will think of a good explanation."

Marsh led the three men up to the mine, and Spivey and Dillon stepped out to greet them. "Hey Marsh, who you got there?"

"Dillon, you remember Clady here from town. These other two gentlemen are also members of the peace committee. Clady you remember Dillon here don't you?"

"Yes, but who is this other man, and where is Porter?"

Marsh was sure Clady would be wondering who Spivey was. So he had thought of a story on the way up to the mine. "This is Spivey, he is Porter's cousin. He came up here to notify us that Porter's father was dying, and he was asking to see his son before he died. Porter left for Santa Fe, and Spivey here decided to stay on and help. As you can see we have got the process down. Dillon, reach down there next to the sluice and pull up a sack of that gold dust. Let Mr. Clady see the results of our labor."

"Looks like Two Time Benny was wrong about this place being played out. I can see you have put in some hard work. We're sorry to have bothered you, and we'll be returning to town now. If you hear of any trouble make sure to let us know."

"Sure thing Clady. You gents have a safe ride back."

Satisfied that Marsh and his men were working the mine, and not having seen any sign of the man fitting Hickey's description, the three men rode away.

Flint rode up beside Clady. "Dan, I don't like the looks of that bunch. Something ain't right, how did that Spivey fellow know where to find them?"

"I agree with you Flint, but we can't prove anything yet, and I didn't want to get into a gunfight. If Hickey was there, he was probably watching us from the cabin. Let's keep an eye on them and spread Hickey's and Porter's descriptions around." They were silent for the rest of the ride.

"That was quick thinking Marsh, telling them about Porter's father dying, and Spivey being his cousin."

"Yeah Boss, but I'm not sure they bought the whole story."

"Maybe not, but it should buy us some time. You three continue to work the mine. Porter and I will scout the large company mines. If any more visitors show up while we're out, place your red neckerchief on the porch railing. That way we will know not to ride in unexpectedly."

Chapter 16

As best as I could figure, I left the cave two days ago. The delirium that had set in from my weakened condition was getting worse. Other than being aware that I was on a travois being pulled by Sallie, I had no idea of where I was, or what direction I was headed. The last thing I remembered was my travois being stopped by something.

When I opened my eyes I was looking up through a hole, and the sun was peeking through at me. It took awhile before I finally realized I was laying inside a teepee. Slowly the cobwebs cleared in my mind, and I remembered falling over the side of a cliff.

A few minutes later an Arapaho squaw entered the teepee carrying a calf skin filled with water. I grunted something out trying to speak, but I'm not really sure what I said, or if she could even understand me. My tongue was swollen and filled my mouth. She knelt down beside me and held the calf skin while I drank. After quenching my immediate thirst, she spoke as she stood up to leave. "I will go and bring the Chief."

Some of the braves knew that I was blood brother to Grey Wolf, Chief of the whole Arapaho Nation. When the big Indian entered the teepee, I couldn't believe my eyes. I was looking straight into the face of Grey Wolf. After having some more water my tongue no longer filled my mouth, and I was able to talk somewhat normal. "Hello my brother, am I ever happy to see you. Am I back at the ranch?"

"No, the tribe was worried about you when you didn't return with any meat as you had promised. They went out to search for you, and after finding you hurt and dying they sent for me. I brought my Medicine Man to heal you. Are you able to move your legs yet?"

"I tried moving them, but I'm still only able to sit up and use my arms. I think I am paralyzed from the legs down."

"Can you tell me what happened to you?"

"I'm not certain, but I think I was bushwhacked, and they left me for dead. If it wasn't for your people finding me, I wouldn't be alive. The best I can recollect, it had been about three weeks after being shot before I passed out for good. How long have I been here?"

"Five days. Your guns are laying over there and we have your mule and Blue. Do you want we should track these men who have done this to you and kill them?"

"No, this is personal Grey Wolf. I will take care of them after I am up and moving again."

It has now been over two weeks since the Arapaho found Logan and brought him back to camp. Since regaining consciousness, the Medicine Man has force fed Logan a nasty tasting broth twice a day. Apparently, it was made out of some kind of cactus juice. Each time after feeding him the broth, the Medicine man would have a squaw massage and bend Logan's legs for at least an hour. As time passed Logan began to give up all hope that he would ever walk again. Then one morning he stretched out to relieve his stiffness, and realized that his legs had moved.

At first I thought it was my imagination. But after sitting up, I tried to bend the leg that had been gashed above the knee. I was able to bring it up to my chest with the help of my hands. I repeated the act with my other leg, getting the same results. The whole camp heard my blood curdling scream. The Medicine Man and Grey Wolf came running into the tent to see what had happened.

I was laughing, and the Medicine Man looked down to see me bending my legs at the knees. Picking me up, the Medicine Man supported me with his shoulders and helped me outside. Still too weak to stand on my own, they made me a pair of crutches. Although I still couldn't walk without crutches, it was a great feeling to know I wouldn't be paralyzed the rest of my life.

For the next four days, I walked around the entire camp on my crutches. Each day putting more weight on my legs for support. I even took time to visit Blue and Sallie. Thanks to the excellent care by the Arapaho over the past couple of weeks, I had regained most of my strength, and all of the weight I had lost. They continued to give me daily massages, strengthening the muscle tone in my legs. After the fifth day of walking around on crutches I was able to toss them aside and walk on my own.

That evening while sitting around the fire I told Grey Wolf about Gideon, and how Bart Hickey had shot and left him for dead. I know he didn't need my advice, but I warned him to make sure his people stayed away from the mining camps.

After two more days of healing I packed up, and began thanking all those that had tended over me. Grey Wolf wished me well, and before letting me ride out he gave me a Henry repeater. "This is one of the rifles you gave me from your battle with Bellows. I think you will have need of it."

"Thanks Grey Wolf, I will visit your camp when I return to the ranch." Riding out I headed back to the cave to search the area where I had been bushwhacked for sign. Hopefully I could find some clues as to who shot me. Even though in my mind, I was certain it was Hickey, or one of his men, that had shot me. But not one to kill an innocent person I needed to be sure. I arrived back at the cave around dusk of the second day out from the Arapaho camp. It was too late to cut for sign, so I made camp inside the cave for the night.

The next morning I rode down to the point where I had been shot and fallen over the cliff. I could see where my fall had been stopped by a large outcropping of rock. If not for that I would have fell further and undoubtedly died. I decided to climb down and search for my lost revolver. After searching for about an hour I found it lying between a couple of rocks. Aside from the handle being scratched up it was fine. Climbing back up I emptied the revolver, reloaded it with fresh cartridges and placed it in my saddlebags.

Riding up to the top of the ridge where I believe the shot had come, I dismounted and scouted for some evidence of who shot me. It was just as I suspected. All around the area were clear prints of three horses. One with a cut in the rear shoe, and another with a star design in the front hoof. There was no question about who bushwhacked me. Hickey and his men had tracked me for the sole purpose of killing me.

The odds of five against one were not so great, at least for me, but it was still wise for me to remember that they are seasoned killers. From here on I would have to stay alert. There was still a lot I had to know before I could ride back into Tin Cup and hunt them down. Besides, I was still a stranger as far as the town's people are concerned, so I can't just go back and start a shooting war. Not without putting myself under suspicion of being a claim jumper. I had to return to our mine first, and make sure Gideon and Charlie are safe. Hopefully they can fill me in on what has been happening during my absence.

Chapter 17

Dan wanted to discuss what he and the other two members of the town's peace keeping committee saw out at Two Time benny's mine. "Emmitt, Flint, meet me over at Mabel's after stabling your horses."

Emmitt was tired and really wanted to get home to his wife. "Dan, can't we get together tomorrow morning and discuss this over breakfast?"

"Sure, I am a little tired myself. I will see you both in the morning."

Hickey and Porter were sitting their horses on the side of the mountain overlooking the Parrish mine. They had been there just over an hour watching the miners activities. As far as they could tell, there were thirty men working inside the mine, and eight men with rifles walking guard. The guards were placed so that they overlapped the entrances to the three mine shafts. It was apparent someone down there had a background in engineering, probably Parrish himself since it was his mine. They had three different shafts working at the same time. Two led into the side of the mountain and one went straight down. Covering the shaft going down was a large A-frame supporting an elaborate pulley system. The shafts going into the mountain had a rail system using large draft horses pulling oversized wooded carts. There were an additional five men working the ore with some sort of crusher.

Porter was always one to state the obvious. "Boss, we can't carry that ore away. Why are we targeting this mine?"

"See that crusher, they are breaking that ore down. They are either selling the smaller chunks of ore, or separating the gold. Either way, were only after the cash they have, not the ore or the gold. Sooner or later one or more of those men are going to ride to Tin Cup and sell it. When that happens we will follow them, and steal the cash on their way back."

"Don't you think they would have more cash down there at the mine?"

"Yes, but we will need the other men to attack the mine. For now we will satisfy ourselves with taking the day's earnings."

They didn't have to wait long before three men saddled up and rode out, leading a mule packing the day's gold to Tin Cup. "Boss we could kill them on the way into town and sell the gold ourselves."

"No we can't. There is no way we could explain that much gold. And our mine doesn't produce anything that rich. Besides when the men didn't return they would track that mule right to us."

Hickey and Porter pulled up into a small stand of trees outside of Tin Cup where they could watch the three men pass. "Boss, I could go into town and keep an eye on them. Make sure they don't return by some other route."

"No! Clady might see you. You're supposed to be in Santa Fe visiting your dying father remember?"

"Oh yeah, I forgot."

"Well don't forget it again."

The three men went straight to the assay office. Twenty minutes after hauling in the packs full of gold they mounted up and headed out of town.

"Come on Porter, we will hit them half way between town and the mine." Hickey and Porter set up on top of a knoll that overlooked the trail where it narrowed. "The riders will have to string out in single file here. When they come even with us, you take out the last man that's leading the mule. I will take the lead man. I don't care which one of us gets the one in the middle."

The men were riding easy in the saddle. They never experienced trouble before, and didn't have reason to expect any today. It was just as Hickey had figured, they moved into single file to get through the narrow trail. When all three of them were strung out in single file, and in front of the knoll, the shots rang out. Seeing the man in front of him fall from his saddle, the second man spurred his horse into the trees to go around his fallen partner. He had heard the report of two shots. He had no doubt that his friend Willie behind him was dead also. Then he felt the two bullets searing through his right shoulder and left side. Falling forward he grabbed his horse's mane, and somehow was able to stay in the saddle.

"Boss, we both hit that third man. He has to be dead."

"We can't be sure, let's get down there and get that cash before he returns with help." They did a quick search for the third man, but couldn't find him. There was plenty of blood where the rider had been hit, but not finding the body they had to believe he was still alive. The first man was carrying ten thousand dollars. The last man only had a few gold coins in is vest, amounting to no more than his wages most likely. Moving quickly they stole the money and rode back to the cabin.

Wheeler rode up to the Parrish mine, falling off his saddle and hitting the dirt hard. Parrish barked out orders. "Johnny, grab a couple other men and carry Wheeler into the office. Josh, ride into town and bring the doctor, and Clady if you can find him."

Inside the cabin Parrish was hovering over Wheeler removing his shirt. "Wheeler what happened?"

Weak from the loss of blood, all Wheeler got out was, "Ambushed, Slick and Willie are dead." Then he lost consciousness.

Parrish washed and dressed the wounds as best he could. All he could do now was wait for the doctor to arrive. He sent his foreman to the mine shafts to put everyone on high alert for an attack.

Josh, Clady and the doctor rode at a gallop to the Parrish mine. On the way there they stopped at the ambush site, and tied the bodies of the dead men over their horses to take them back to Parrish. None of the men knew anything about tracking, and had made no attempt to look for any sign of the killers. In fact, by walking all around and retrieving the dead men and their horses, they wiped out all sign of the robbers around the trail with their own tracks.

The doctor was able to remove the bullets from Wheeler. Neither wound was life threating, but he had lost a lot of blood and remained unconscious. Clady decided to wait around until Wheeler came around so he could question him. In the meantime, he informed Parrish about Hickey, and gave him a description of both Hickey and Porter. "Mr. Parrish, a lot of the small miners have gone missing, and a single man fitting Hickey's description has resold their claims. I'd be willing to bet it was Hickey that ambushed your men and stole the cash." A couple hours later Wheeler came to, but he couldn't describe the ambushers since he had never seen them.

With Wheeler awake and no longer in danger of dying, Clady and the doctor left. "Doc, I have a feeling your work is about to increase."

"I hope you're wrong Dan, but it sounds like this Hickey fellow is bad news. What else do you know about him?"

"There are stories about him and his gang killing a lot of miners and the Sheriff of Pueblo back in 1858 and 59'. I wish we had an experienced lawman. I don't think the town's peace committee can handle a gang like his."

Hickey and Porter arrived back at the cabin, and Hickey sent Porter up to the mine to get the others for a meeting. "I want you all to stay around the cabin when we're not out on a raid."

Marsh was interested in what the take was from the Parrish mine. "How much did you get today Boss?"

"Ten thousand dollars. They must be taking their find into town every week. Meaning the big payday is stashed at the mine. With what we saw and how long they have been operating, I am thinking they should have as much as three hundred thousand being held at the mine."

"Whooee! We could leave the area with that much money for sure."

"Shut up Dillon. They will be looking for us now. In the meantime, we will hit the other mines first, and raid the Parrish mine last."

Chapter 18

Riding up to Gideon's mine I noticed something wrong. The tent was no longer visible and I couldn't see any activity. I started to hail the mine and let Charlie and Gideon know I was coming, but I couldn't be sure who was up there, if anyone. Yelling out would put any claim jumpers on notice of my arrival. Dismounting I tied Blue and Sallie to a tree. After switching over to my moccasins, I slowly started creeping up on the mine. They had built a protective wall as I had suggested. Just as I was about to open the gate, I heard some movement inside the mine. It was too dark to see inside the shaft and to determine who was moving around.

The hinges on the gate were made out of wood and leather, so it should open without squeaking. Opening the gate just enough to slide through, I low crawled up to the side of the shaft's opening. Peeking into the mine I could make out Charlie standing by the fire. There didn't seem to be anything wrong, so I decided to have a little fun. Moving back to the wall I lowered myself down behind it and yelled. "Freeze, I got you covered." Charlie turned in fright, and without aiming he fired his rifle at the voice.

Gideon came running from the back of the mine. "Charlie, what's wrong, are we under attack?"

Logan was giggling. "Careful there old man, you wouldn't want to kill one of your partners now would you?"

"Dag nab it Logan, you scared the stuffing's out of me. Where have you been?"

"I'll tell you everything after I take care of my horses."

With the animals fed and brushed, I went back up to the mine. Charlie showed me the progress they had made. "I am impressed, you two have put in a lot of work during my absence. You did a fine job on that wall you built for defense. Short of being blown up by dynamite it doesn't look like its coming down."

"Thanks, we took you serious about building it with Hickey being in the area. You took an awful long time to hunt a couple Elk."

"Hickey must have learned of my association with you Gideon. He and his men bushwhacked me and I was temporarily paralyzed. The Arapaho found me tethered behind Sallie, and none too soon either. I probably wouldn't have lasted another day."

"If you were bushwhacked how do you know it was Hickey?"

"I went back to where I was shot and found the sign of his, and that other horse's shoe prints."

Showing them the notch running the length of the back of my head, I told them the whole story of my fight for survival.

Charlie stared at Logan with the understanding that any other man would have probably died. "Lucky you bent over just at that moment. Somebody important is looking over you."

"I guess, but it sounds as if Hickey is back up to his old habit of claim jumping. His kind wouldn't be here for anything else."

Charlie wanted Logan to stay at the mine with him and Gideon. But he knew Logan wouldn't rest until he hunted Hickey down, and repaid him for the haircut. "Logan I gave that fellow Clady a description of Hickey, but no one in town has seen hide nor hair of him."

"Hickey won't reveal himself if he can help it. If he did, the town would run him out of the territory before he could do any more damage."

"I suppose, but Clady and his peace keeping committee are no match for Hickey's gang. What are we going to do?"

"We aren't going to do anything. I want you and Gideon to stay here and continue working the mine. I will take care of Hickey."

The next day, while Charlie and Gideon worked inside the mine, Logan cleared the trees closest to the mine to open up a better field of fire. Then he set some traps farther out in the trees for anyone sneaking around. He marked the traps with a small circle of stones. The stones were fashioned into his ranch brand of the Circle M. He relayed this information to Charlie and Gideon so they would not walk into the traps themselves. The traps would not kill anyone instantly, but they would severely cut a man's foot or leg, and most likely cause him to scream out in pain involuntarily.

"Charlie, I want you two stay out of the woods unless absolutely necessary. Now give me my rifle back. Here is another one to replace it."

"What's the difference?"

"Mine holds eighteen shots. This older model only holds twelve."

With a quizzical look on his face Charlie said, "I didn't even notice."

Logan started laughing, "Well, the way you shoot, I don't think the extra six shots would have helped you anyway."

"Very funny. How do you plan on getting Hickey without looking like a renegade yourself?"

"I am going to take Clady up on that sheriff's job."

"That will make Clady a happy man. I could tell he didn't want to tackle Hickey himself, and he seems to think pretty highly of you."

The next morning Logan saddled up Dusty to ride into Tin Cup. "You two make sure one of you stands guard at all times. During the day take 2-hour shifts. That is about all you can stay focused. At night you can stand 4-hour shifts." Sallie was trailing behind as usual with Blue and a small pack of supplies strapped to the pack saddle. He still wanted to make it look like he was returning from the hunting trip, and to keep anyone from asking too many questions. To sell the story, he once again rode into town from the north.

As he rode through town, everyone was stepping out of their places of business to watch. No one was feeling safe around strangers, especially with the miners being robbed and killed. Aside from Clady and the bartender, no one really knew Logan, or why he was in the territory. Recognizing him from being in town before, and not fitting the description of Hickey, they all went back to attend to their own business. Logan dismounted in front of the Gold Dust saloon and entered, he carefully looked around to see if any of Hickey's men were inside. "Bartender, I'll have a beer and a shot of whiskey."

"Coming right up Mr. Hayes. Haven't seen you for quite a while, did you have any luck?"

Before he could answer Clady stepped up beside him. "Hello again, Mr. Hayes, isn't it?"

"Yes sir. You have a good memory for names."

"Comes with the territory."

"Bartender, give my friend Mr. Clady here a cold beer."

"How was your hunting trip?"

"To tell you the truth I got sidetracked a little. Seems someone didn't like me hunting up in the Pass."

Logan showed Clady the groove in the back of his head, and Clady let out a small gasp. "That's a pretty nasty cut, how did that happen?"

"I was bushwhacked. I have reason to believe Hickey and his men are the culprits. Haven't seen him around have you?"

"No, but we have reason to believe he is behind a rash of claim jumping that has been going on. What makes you think Hickey was behind the ambush on you?"

"I found the hoof prints belonging to his and his partner's horses where it happened. One has a cut in the rear hoof, and the other has the design of a star in his right hoof. I believe the horse with the star print belongs to Hickey. Have you seen any tracks matching that description?"

"I am not much of a tracker, Mr. Hayes. Can't say I would have noticed even if they were around. What are your plans now? You plan on leaving the mountains, or are you going back up into the Pass to continue your hunt?"

Logan took a long deep drink of his beer. "Please, call me Logan, and I am glad you asked. I was hoping that job of sheriff you offered me was still open. If it is I would like to accept it."

"Mr. Hayes, I mean Logan, you're hired. And you can call me Dan."

"Good, let's finish our drinks Dan, and you can show me to my cabin." After finishing their drinks Clady walked Logan down to the edge of town to his temporary living quarters. Logan was pleased to find out the cabin had a small corral to hold his horses, and a shed to keep his tack dry. This would be helpful in allowing him to enter and leave town without being noticed.

The next day Clady introduced Logan to the rest of the peace keeping committee, and to several of the local business owners. While they didn't know much about Logan, they were pleased to have an actual sheriff in town for protection.

"Dan I would appreciate it if you would ride out with me tomorrow, and introduce me to the mine owners. I wouldn't like to get shot being mistaken for a thief. A formal introduction by you would help prevent that, and hopefully get them to open up and talk to me."

"It would be my pleasure. I have been wanting to make the rounds again anyway."

"Great, before you leave maybe you could tell me where this latest attack I heard about took place?" After Clady gave Logan directions on how to get out to the ambush site, he headed back to his office. Logan mounted up and rode out to where the Parrish riders had been ambushed to search for clues.

With Clady's men and horses having walked all over the place, Logan couldn't pick out any distinguishing tracks. Turning around, he focused his attention farther out from the trail to the surrounding terrain. He spied the knoll up to his left. Based on his experience it offered the best place for an ambush on anyone traveling along the trail. Stepping down from Dusty, Logan walked around looking for sign. It didn't take long before he found what he was looking for, the hoof prints of Hickey's and his partner's horses. He also found a cartridge from a Sharps 54 caliber rifle. Most likely the same rifle that was used to shoot him, based on the distance of the shot. He picked up the empty cartridge and headed back to town.

Chapter 19

Logan and Clady had visited almost all the mines by day's end. "Logan, we only have three mines left to visit. Two which I believe were resold to the newcomers by Hickey."

"What about the third one?"

"It was sold to some cowboys up from Santa Fe, by the previous owner, Two Time Benny."

"Can I talk to this Two Time Benny?"

"No, it seems he left the territory."

"Did anyone talk to him before he left?"

"No, which was mighty surprising to most of us that have been around since the beginning. Benny was well liked, and it wasn't like him to leave without saying goodbye. Besides, they are pulling some good color out of that mine. Benny was too good a miner to have believed his mine was played out like they said. It wasn't like him to pull up stakes and quit on a good strike. I also find it a little strange that his was the only mine not sold by the man fitting Hickey's description."

"Why don't we visit those other two mines and then head back to town. I want to visit Two Time Benny's mine later on my own."

"Fine with me. I don't mind telling you I don't much like that crowd mining Benny's claim anyway."

After visiting the last two mines as scheduled they headed back to town. On the way back Logan asked, "What about to the southwest of town? We haven't visited anyone over in that direction."

"There aren't any mines over that way. There have been a few who have tried panning over on the Taylor River, but they didn't have any luck. So no one else has had any desire to waste their time over in that direction. Especially with all the rich fields having been found to the north and east of town."

Logan was glad to hear no one had found success on the Taylor River. It reduced the opportunity for anyone finding Gideon's mine. The town didn't have an actual sheriff's office. So for the next couple of days, Logan spent most of his time getting to know the town's residents. Otherwise he could be found at the Gold Dust. Usually drinking coffee and watching who came and went, and listening to the local gossip.

Logan was having lunch at Mabel's when Clady strolled in and walked over to him. "Good afternoon Dan."

"Good afternoon Sheriff. I thought you might like to know, the one called Marsh from Benny's mine just came in to sell some gold over at the assay office."

"Thanks, do you think he knows I am the sheriff?"

"Not unless the clerk over at the assay office has told him. But I can't think of any reason he would."

Logan left the rest of his meal sitting untouched at the café, and walked over to the saloon. The bartender was wiping down the bar as he entered, "Pike, has anyone been in here in the last fifteen minutes?"

"Not a soul Sheriff."

"Good, but for now call me Mr. Hayes instead of Sheriff."

"Whatever you want, any reason why?"

"I will tell you later." Logan walked over and sat down at his usual table.

It wasn't but a few minutes later that Marsh stepped into the saloon. He came to an abrupt halt upon seeing Logan. He started to turn around and leave, but thought it would make him look suspicious. "Howdy Pike, how about a cold one?"

"Coming right up Marsh." Logan heard the name and knew he was looking at the right man. The bartender returned with Marsh's beer. "Looks like you boys have done pretty good for yourselves. Guess Two Time's mine wasn't played out after all."

Marsh hesitated to reply, his attention was on the mirror as he was watching Logan in the reflection. "I guess, but it's been a lot of hard work. It isn't just sitting out in the open you know." Marsh finished his beer and left.

Logan could now put a face and name to at least one of Hickey's men. He followed Marsh out and watched him ride out of town. Logan made a point of noticing Marsh had a Henry repeater in the rifle boot. Meaning most likely that he wasn't the one who shot him. He confirmed this by checking the tracks of Marsh's horse. The hooves didn't have a cut or star print in them. As usual though, Logan registered the horses print and gait into his memory.

Marsh hustled back to the cabin. "I'm telling you Boss, it was him."

"It couldn't be, I saw Porter blow the back of his head away. And besides, where has he been for the last month and a half if he was alive? The only doctor around these parts is in Tin Cup, and we would have heard about him showing up with half his head shot off."

"I don't know boss, but I am certain it was him. I even saw that big Dun he rides tied up outside of Mabel's café."

"Did you see any sign of the two old timers?"

"No."

"Well, we can't just ride into town and kill him. Do you think he recognized you?"

"I don't know how he could have since he has never seen me before. Besides, he just sat at that table drinking coffee like I wasn't even there."

"Let's keep an eye out for him. If he comes snooping around you all know what to do. There isn't any other law in town to help him, and those cowards following Clady won't do anything. We should be safe out here at the mine. Marsh, what's the tally on the gold you and the boys have worked out of the mine?"

"Counting what we sold today it comes to fifteen thousand."

"So adding that to want we have taken from the independent miners, and that old coot in the gorge, we have around sixty thousand total. I want at least two hundred thousand before we leave. That's twenty thousand a piece for each of you, everyone okay with that?"

Dillon was not happy with the new split. "Boss, that leaves you with a hundred thousand. That doesn't seem fair."

Hickey drew his pistol and pointed it right into Dillon's face. "I get a larger share because I am the brains and the leader of this outfit. Do you want to challenge my decision?"

Dillon knew Hickey would shoot him if he gave the wrong answer. "No Boss, the splits fair I guess."

"What about the rest of you, any complaints?" Each of the others replied with a resounding no. "Marsh I want you to stop working the mine. From now on we will stick to robbing the other mines until we are ready to pull out."

Hickey knew a couple of the men might get killed in the raids to follow, increasing each one's share. But, one thing he knew for sure, he was going to kill Dillon for challenging him before they were finished. "Porter, saddle our horses, you and I are going to scout the Youngblood mine today."

Logan mounted up and rode out of town to the northeast. Clady watched him leave and figured he was headed out to Two Time Benny's mine. But he didn't know what one man alone could do against Hickey and his gang.

After leaving town, Logan swung to the south to circle around and approach Two Time Benny's cabin from the east. When he figured he was within half a mile from the mine he dismounted. He merely dropped the reigns to Dusty in case he had to make a quick get away

As he reached the top of the ridge overlooking the cabin, he saw two men riding away. There was no reason for him to follow them. He was just conducting reconnaissance of the place to determine their numbers, and see what kind of defenses they've put in place. Logan had been watching for approximately two hours when he saw four men come out of the cabin. Counting the two who rode out that made a total of six, and he could now recognize four of them. Hickey must have been one of the two who rode out, because none of the four men that came out of the cabin had blond hair. Logan mounted up, he felt sure he would recognize Hickey when he saw him. That left only one unknown man. The one with the Sharps.

Not getting to finish his lunch when Marsh had come into town, Logan's stomach was growling, so he rode straight to Mable's to get something to eat. Clady had been awaiting his return, so he strolled over to see what Logan had learned, if anything. "Logan, mind if I sit?"

"Just so long as you don't give me any more news to interrupt my meal."

"Nothing like that, I was just curious about where you went, and if you found out anything more about the killing of Parrish's men."

Logan filled Clady in on finding the ambush site while he ate, and about what he had seen out at Two Time Benny's. "I think they are planning to escalate their attacks. Hickey and another man were riding out as I arrived. I believe they went out to scout their next target."

"What makes you believe that?"

"I noticed they have quit working Benny's mine. Marsh must have come in to sell the last of their diggings. Dan, I am going to ride out to each of the mines and give them some advice on how to strengthen their security measures. I will start with the Youngblood mine."

Chapter 20

Joey was leaning against the rail of the corral watching the ranch hands break in the horses brought in from the range when four men rode into the yard. Joey immediately removed the leather hammer thong holding down his pistol. He was staring directly into the eyes of Quentin Bellows, the older brother of James Bellows.

Quentin spoke first, "Look here boy's, it's Joey. I wasn't exactly sure what I expected to find here kid, but it surely wasn't you. I thought you were dead. How is it you survived McCart's revenge, and forty plus other men didn't? Including my brother."

Joey wasn't sure if he should draw or speak. "What do you want here Quentin? I thought you were locked up in a Federal Prison over in Missouri for life."

Quentin smiled, "My boys here thought I had spent enough time in prison and broke me out. How is it you have come to work for the man who killed my brother? Who, if I remember correctly, you were riding for when he stood against McCart. It was obvious Quentin was unhappy with finding Joey alive, let alone working for the man who killed his brother.

"McCart offered the last five men standing with your brother the chance to leave and live. Glen and Pete, along with myself, accepted his offer."

Quentin was starting to let his anger show. "Well that doesn't explain how you ended up here working for McCart, and what happened to Glen and Pete?"

The men breaking horses had now moved to the rail of the corral to listen, but they were unarmed. Joey knew he couldn't rely on them for any help. "The Federal Marshall, James Brodie, is a friend of Mr. McCart and he gave me a recommendation. Brodie killed Glen and Pete in Junction City when they decided to draw on him."

"Well kid, I came here to kill McCart. I guess I'll just have to take care of you at the same time for your betrayal. I notice you released your hammer thong. As I remember it, you weren't to fast with that hog leg. You must think your fast enough to out draw me now do you?"

"Mr. McCart has worked with me Quentin. I'm not the same young boy you used to know. Maybe I won't get you all, but I will blow you out of the saddle before it's all over."

Lisa McCart had been listening just inside the door of the house. After hearing the name Quentin Bellows she had froze with fear. Regaining her composure, she reached up beside the door and pulled down the Henry repeater hanging on the wall. At the same time Randy had emerged from the barn and was quietly walking up behind the four men sitting their horses. He was carrying his Greener shotgun, and slipped up closer without them noticing him.

Quentin was irritated by Joey's bravado, and it showed in his voice. "Where is McCart and his sister?"

Joey made a mistake that he would realize later, and told him. "Mr. McCart is hunting up in the Rockies."

"Well kid, I'll just have to satisfy myself by killing you for now, and deal with the McCart's afterwards."

"If you want to live Quentin, I would just turn that horse of yours around and ride to Mexico."

Without turning his head, Joey had seen Lisa step out of the house. They all heard the distinct sound as she chambered a round in the rifle. "I don't think you will be doing either sir. If I was you I would take Joey's advice and ride on."

Quentin turned his head to look at the woman who had just spoken. "You must be the little sister I've heard so much about. Looks like I'll at least ride away having killed you along with this coward."

Just then Randy spoke out, "I don't think you will be killing anyone today Bellows." As Quentin turned in the saddle to look at the man speaking from behind him, Randy cocked the triggers on the double barrel shotgun.

Quentin knew the odds of winning a gunfight had now changed against him. With Joey in front and the girl on the porch he hadn't been too concerned, but with that shotgun pointed at their backs he couldn't hope to win. "Seems like we are at a stand off. Alright, we'll ride out, but I'll be back after I take care of Logan." Quentin tipped his hat to Lisa as they turned and rode away.

Joey knew Quentin couldn't be trusted. After Bellows and his men had ridden out of sight, he turned to the corral where the bronc riders were still standing. "Nash, saddle up and follow them. Make sure they keep riding. When you determine what direction they're headed, and you're sure they are not doubling back, ride back here and let me know."

"Will do Joey, how long do you want me to trail them?"

"A minimum of two days, I want to make sure they don't circle back. And I think I made a mistake by telling them Mr. McCart was hunting up in the Rockies. Now get moving."

Lisa knows her brother can protect himself, so she turned her attention to the ranch hands. "From now on I want everyone to wear their side arms and carry a rifle in your scabbard. You need to be ready for trouble at all times."

It was one of the men in the corral that spoke up. "But Miss McCart, we can't break these horses wearing guns."

"Forget the horses, we can break them later. I want everyone to stay close in case there is any more trouble from Bellows and his men. If you have to ride out and work the cattle, make sure there are at least three of you riding together at all times."

Nash returned six days later. "Joey, I followed them all the way to Big Timbers, and slipped down to their camp to listen. You were right, they are headed to the Rockies to find Mr. McCart."

"Thanks Nash, take care of your horse and get something to eat. Randy, I have to go find Mr. McCart and warn him."

Randy couldn't let Joey leave. He was the only fast gun on the ranch and Lisa might need him. "You have to stay here Joey, I will go instead. Before he left, Logan tasked you with protecting Miss McCart, and that is exactly what you are going to do. If Quentin decides to back track, you are the only one that can stand against him."

"You're right Randy. Cut through the ranch and ride through Arapaho territory. It will bring you into the Rockies from the north and you will be able to avoid Quentin and his men."

Randy was saddling his horse and packing a mule with supplies when Lisa came out to talk to him. "Randy, are you sure about this? We have a lot of younger men that can make the ride."

"I still got a lot left in me ma'am. Besides, none of the other men know your brother's habits better than I do. Plus the Arapaho know me. It will be easier and faster for me to find him instead of someone else."

"I guess so. You take care of yourself and stay out of Mr. Bellows sights. He won't forget you covered him with that shotgun." Randy thanked her for her concern and mounted up.

Two days later Randy rode into the Arapaho camp on the banks of the Pawnee river. Chief Grey Wolf told Randy about Logan having been ambushed, and how they nursed him back to health up on the Arkansas. Randy was certain Logan would remain up in the Pass. What concerned him was who could have ambushed Logan. It couldn't have been Quentin Bellows. He was still in prison at that time.

Randy left the Arapaho camp at sunup. With this new information about someone else hunting Logan, Randy was reconsidering his decision to ride out alone to warn Logan of Quentin Bellows. He also wondered if it might not have been better to let Joey come instead with this new development of additional killers chasing Logan. Not knowing who the new threat was, Randy knew he would have to proceed cautiously. If he meets anyone on the trail, he must not give away the fact that he knows or is looking for Logan.

Randy spent the night camped on the Arkansas River. Although he was taking a more direct route to Cottonwood Pass, he doubted he would get there before Bellows. His only hope was that he could find and warn Logan before Quentin could locate him.

Chapter 21

Even after the attack on Parrish's men, there were no guards posted at the Youngblood mine. I was able to ride straight up to the office without a challenge. I had been sitting in my saddle outside the office for about three minutes before a man finally stepped out to greet me. "Hello Sheriff, can I help you?"

"Yes, I would like to speak with Mr. Youngblood."

"Step down off your horse and come in and sit. Mr. Youngblood is down at the mine, I'll go get him for you."

"If you don't mind, I'd prefer to walk along with you."

"I think that would be alright, let's go."

Logan only saw two guards, and they were posted at the opening of the mine. Logan and his escort were a hundred yards into the mine shaft when Mr. Youngblood greeted them. "Hello Sheriff, is there a problem?"

"No, I wanted to come talk to you about your security measures. I expect Hickey to step up his activity and start raiding the larger mines. I was hoping you would give me a tour of your operations."

"Sure, I'm willing to listen to any advice you may have to help protect our investment."

Aside from the two guards outside the mine entrance, there were two guards inside the mine. One stayed at the work area, and one accompanied the carts carrying the ore out of the mine. The two guards inside the mine were there to keep the employees from stealing nuggets they could place in their pockets.

After walking the perimeter of the mine they returned to the office. "How about a cup of coffee, while we talk Sheriff?"

"Thanks, don't mind if I do. There's nothing I like better than a good hot cup of coffee."

"What do you think of our operation?"

"Your operations are laid out very well, and it appears you have set up your materials and men to work efficiently. However, your security is not very good at all."

"Sheriff, I can tell you we have had no stealing by the workers with our guards posted. Our security has served our purposes well up to now. Why do you believe them to be inadequate?"

"I agree with you sir. With regard to internal thefts, your security is fine. But for repelling an organized attack from outside the mine, your security is severely lacking."

"I see, to tell you the truth I hadn't really thought of an external assault. We have enough men that I really didn't think anyone would attempt an attack against us."

"Numbers don't account for a whole lot against a seasoned gang of outlaws. Mr. Youngblood, would you mind my asking where your gold and cash are kept?"

"Micah, show the sheriff our safe." Micah came around from his desk and pulled away the throw rug. Bending down he grabbed a ring bolted to the floor and opened a trap door. Sitting under the floor boards was a large safe.

Logan knew the purpose of the safe being hidden below the floor, but he also knew it would not prevent the likes of Hickey from finding it and stealing its content. "Mr. Youngblood, I know you believe your valuables are safe hidden under the floor, but you couldn't be more wrong. First off, Hickey knows you will keep the safe somewhere in the office. He has been claim jumping since 58', that I know of, and he knows all the tricks. Also, I notice none of your men inside the office are armed, can I ask why?"

"No particular reason, but my armed guards outside reduce any temptation. Besides, I would trust these three men with my life. They have been with me for several years and are very loyal. Along with myself, no one other than these men know the location of the safe."

Logan slowly surveyed the room, looking closely at each man as he did. "Gentlemen, raise your hand if you are willing to die to protect the location of the safe." Not a single man raised his hand. "You see Mr. Youngblood, while they may be fiercely loyal, they are not willing to die to keep the location of the safe a secret. Oh, maybe against the local turncoat worker, but not against a ruthless killer like Hickey."

"You have proven your point Sheriff, what do you suggest I do?"

"First, take the two guards protecting the entrance to the mine and move them up here to the office. Bandits will not be interested in the ore inside the mine, it's too heavy to carry. They are more interested in your cash. So there is no reason to protect the mines entrance. I also noticed the guards do not carry any extra ammunition. Supply each of them with a box of shells. Have your men build a firing wall around the porch. This will allow the guards to protect themselves against incoming fire. Lastly, I would arm these three men with revolvers to back up the guards should an attack come."

"All excellent ideas Sherriff. I will do as you have suggested. If I didn't know any better I would think you've done this before."

"Other than the layout, a mine isn't any different than any other objective. Not that it makes any difference, but I was a Major in the Union Army."

"Very good, any other advice?"

"Yes, pick out six of your mine workers to serve as guards. I am sure some of them also served during the war, and they would probably prefer standing guard as opposed to sweating inside the mine. I will show you where to post them."

Mr. Youngblood expressed his dissatisfaction with reducing his workforce to expand the guard. "Sheriff, that is a third of my workforce. My mining operations will suffer substantially."

"Would you prefer to have a slower production rate, or lose everything?"

"Point well taken, I'll do it."

Before leaving, Logan showed Mr. Youngblood where to post the other three guards. Two would be placed on the perimeter of the compound across from the office and out of sight. Their positions would allow them to catch any marauding riders in a crossfire between them and the guards stationed on the office porch. The third guard was to be posted approximately three hundred yards outside the perimeter to sound the alarm of any approaching threat."

By the time Logan was ready to leave, he had gained the full respect and friendship of Mr. Youngblood. Logan left him with one final piece of advice. "Rotate the guard every six hours. After dark you can discontinue the perimeter guard, and maintain a single guard in the office to raise the alarm."

It has been three days since Hickey scouted the Youngblood operations. He had no idea Logan had visited the mine and persuaded Youngblood to improve his security measures. "Saddle up boys, we should be back by nightfall a lot richer. Marsh, you and Dillon ride in the lead and take out the two guards posted in front of the mine. Then lay down fire and keep the rest of their men pinned inside the mine. Spivey you wait outside the office, and kill anyone who tries to interfere. Cullen, you hold the horses, Porter and I will go inside and get the cash."

It was estimated that the mine had close to fifty thousand dollars cash stored in the safe. They were within two hundred yards of the mine when they heard the shot up on the mountain behind them. Dillon wanted to forget the raid. "Boss, they know we're here, let's get out of here before we're trapped."

"Whoever it is wasn't shooting at us, and there hasn't been any more shots. It's probably just someone out hunting. You and Marsh go in as planned."

Marsh and Dillon rode into the compound firing at the entrance of the mine. Instantly Marsh realized there were no guards posted at the entrance of the shaft. He pulled up just as the volley of fire from the sides took out Dillon. Marsh wheeled his horse around and raced out of the compound. Hickey and the rest of the gang were just about to enter the compound as Marsh came riding out, yelling, "It's a trap, run!".

Back at the cabin Hickey's men were confused and in a heated discussion about what had taken place at the mine. Marsh wasn't happy about riding into a trap. "Hickey, I thought you and

Porter scouted the mine. They were prepared for us and caught us in a crossfire."

"I don't know Marsh. Something caused them to change the positioning of their guards. I'm telling you there were only the two guards outside the mine shaft, and two inside of it, when Porter and I scouted it the other day.

Porter was more concerned about the man left behind. "Marsh, what about Dillon, do you think he is still alive to talk?"

"No way, he was riddled by the bullets from at least three guards. He isn't going to be talking to anyone anymore."

Hickey thought to himself. *"Good, I was going to kill him anyway before we left the Pass. I will not tolerate disobedience."*

Now that the mines are on notice Hickey was going to need more men. "Marsh, I want you to ride into Tin Cup and find some men looking for work. I'm sure I don't have to tell what kind of men I am looking for."

"I understand Boss."

"Keep an eye out for that hunter too, and if you can get some information about him and what he's really doing up here. I don't believe he came all the way up here just to hunt."

Everything in Tin Cup appeared normal as Marsh rode down the street, and he didn't see the hunter's Dun horse anywhere in sight. Stopping at the saloon he was surprised to see all the horses tied up out front. Stepping inside he saw four men standing at the bar. It was obvious they were not miners. Marsh walked over and sat down at a table. "Pike, bring me a beer would ya?"

"Sure thing Marsh."

Pike delivered the beer and Marsh wanted to satisfy his curiosity. Whispering, he asked, "Pike, who are the four toughs at the bar?"

"I don't know, they rode in about a half hour ago, asking if I knew a Mr. McCart. I told them I never heard of him, but by the description they gave me, it sounds a lot like our new sheriff."

"Sheriff, when did Tin Cup get a sheriff?"

"Right after those Parrish riders were robbed and killed."

"What do you now about this new sheriff?"

"Not much, other than his name is Hayes, and he came up into the mountains to hunt Elk."

"Do you know where he came from?"

"If I recall correctly he said he was from Kansas. He stays to himself most of the time and doesn't talk about himself. As far as I can tell, he doesn't seem to interested in mining for gold."

"Anything else you can tell me about this sheriff?"

"Only that Mr. Clady offered him the job a couple months ago when he first hit town, but he declined the offer at that time. Then he shows up about a week ago and accepts the position. He didn't give a reason as to why he changed his mind."

"Thanks Pike, give those gents at the bar another beer on me, and ask them to step over and join me."

Quentin led his men over to the table. "Have a seat gentlemen. My name is Marsh, I would like to talk and offer you a proposition."

Quentin sat directly across from Marsh, and then the rest of his men sat down around the table. "Marsh huh, thanks for the beer. What makes you think you have anything that could interest us?"

"Pike tells me you are looking for a man named McCart?"

"What if we are, what business is it of yours, are you a friend of his'?

"Don't even know him, but from the description you gave the bartender I believe he is the new town sheriff."

"And you think this entitles you to some reward or something?"

"My boss has had trouble with him, and I thought we might be able to join forces."

"I can take care of this sheriff by myself. I don't need any piss-ant miners to help me."

Marsh took offense to the remark, but was to outnumbered to do anything about it. Besides, Hickey wanted hard men to help raid the mines, and these gents definitely fit the bill. "Look here mister, I'm not here to be insulted, and we aren't miners. My boss needs tough men, and I thought you men might want to share a couple hundred thousand dollars. We won't interfere with you and your business with the sheriff.

Quentin's interest was peaked at the thought of a couple hundred thousand dollars. He thought in the end he might be able to take all the loot, and kill McCart in the bargain, but he wanted to know more before committing to anything. "Bartender, bring us a bottle of whiskey and five glasses." After pouring the drinks Quentin returned his focus back to Marsh. "Where is this boss of yours, and what's his name?"

"We have a cabin just northeast of here. My boss' name is Bart Hickey."

"That name doesn't mean anything to me. What about this money you mentioned, and what do we have to do to get it?"

Marsh wasn't sure if he should tell them about the claim jumping, but knew they wouldn't leave with him if he didn't. Lowering his voice, he said, "We are robbing the miners. We have already jumped the small claims and are now going after the big outfits."

"So what do you need us for?"

"Someone has been helping the mines increase their security forces and improve their defenses."

"What's our share if we decide to help?"

"You will have to settle that with Hickey. He makes all the decisions regarding the split."

"I ain't saying yes or no until I talk to Hickey himself. Lets have another drink, and then we can ride out and have a talk with this boss of yours."

Chapter 22

Logan was returning from the Walker mine when he saw the five men riding out the other side of town. He recognized Marsh, but he hadn't seen the other four before. He was sure he didn't know them, but by the way they sat their horses he knew they weren't miners. He had planned on stopping at his place and getting some rest, but after seeing the five men ride out, he decided to ride on down to the saloon and quench his thirst. Chances were that Pike would be able to tell him something about the men who rode out with Marsh.

"Howdy Sherriff, where you been?"

"Just got back from the Walker mine. Pete, I saw four men ride out with Marsh as I rode in, can you tell me anything about them?"

"Not much, they were looking for a feller named McCart."

Logan snapped his head up, he was taken by surprise when he heard his real name. "Did they give you their names, or mention where they're from?"

"No, Marsh bought them a drink, then they sat over there and talked."

"Did they seem to know each other?"

"Didn't seem so, in fact I heard the leader of the four men actually insult Marsh. Called him a piss-ant miner. I thought Marsh was going to draw on him, but he must not have liked the odds.

Come to think of it, that's the first time I ever saw Marsh wearing a gun. Then they ordered a bottle of whiskey, and after some more talking and drinking they all left together. Sherriff, I'm sorry, but I told Marsh you accepted the sheriff's job."

"That's alright Pete, he was bound to find out sooner or later. Thanks for the information. I'll see you later."

"One more thing Sheriff, the leader of those four men described this Mr. McCart to me, and it sounded a whole lot like you."

"Did you tell him that?"

"No, but Marsh heard the description and he might have said something."

It bothered Logan that someone was looking for him under his surname of McCart. That meant they knew his real identity, and was looking for him for some specific reason that wasn't associated with Tin Cup. Logan was certain it wasn't to rekindle a long lost friendship. Pete had described the man, but Logan didn't recall knowing anyone by that description. As hard as Logan tried, he could not think of any reason, or person with a grudge, for hunting him down.

After crossing the Arkansas, Randy visited the Arapaho camp where Logan had been nursed back to health. They had supplied Randy with enough information that he was able to locate the cave Logan had used during his hunt. Entering the cave he found the supplies left by Logan. It was clear though, that no one had used the cave for several weeks. Knowing Logan as he did, he knew Logan would be pursuing his bushwhackers. Tomorrow he would head to Tin Cup and see if he could get any information on Logan's whereabouts. As for tonight, there wasn't any better place to spend it than inside the cave.

Marsh rode up to the cabin with Bellows' gang following behind. Hickey had seen them coming, and had already stepped out onto the porch to greet them. It wasn't difficult for Hickey to determine who the boss of the group was, being the same type of man himself. "Who are these men Marsh?"

Pointing to Quentin, he said, "This is Mr. Bellows and his men. They have come to listen to your proposition. It seems they have some grudge of their own against our hunter."

"Step down gentlemen, come inside and we'll talk over some whiskey."

As the men dismounted, Marsh spoke to Hickey as they entered the cabin. "Boss, it appears our hunter has taken the position of sheriff in Tin Cup."

The news that the hunter was now sheriff of Tin Cup was disturbing to Hickey. After everyone had sat down, Hickey addressed Bellows. "I take it you are leading these men. What brings you so high up into the mountains?"

"My name is Quentin Bellows, and I am searching for the man that killed my younger brother. A man named Logan McCart, have you heard of him?"

"No, should I have?"

"Not really, until his parents were murdered, I don't think anyone knew of him."

"What makes him so special now?"

"He killed my brother and over forty men all by himself getting his revenge."

"Sounds like somebody I would want to avoid, not hunting."

"Well, according to my information, and your man Marsh here, you have already made that mistake."

"What's that supposed to mean?"

"It means you have already tried to kill him, and failed."

"Are you telling me this hunter is the same man you know as McCart?"

"Exactly, I don't know what name he is using up here, but by all accounts and the description Marsh gave me, your hunter and McCart are the same man."

"So, what, you decided to come out here and enlist my help to kill this McCart for you?"

"Don't be foolish, we were told you were going to make us rich."

It was obvious that Hickey and Bellows didn't like each other. But Hickey needed men, and he couldn't really be choosey. No matter his dislike of the man, he could tell Bellows and his men were skilled gun fighters. Not knowing Bellows' history, he was sure he could eliminate him after the raids were completed. Unknown to Hickey, Bellows was having the same thought about eliminating him. Neither man gave a single thought about Logan killing them both.

Bellows had enough of the bantering back and forth regarding McCart. "Why don't you fill me in on your operations so I can decide if I want to buy-in."

Hickey described his plans for hitting the three large mines, and the estimated take of approximately two hundred thousand dollars. Hickey didn't bother to tell him about the sixty plus thousand they were already holding. That didn't make any difference, Bellows already knew he was holding something from the small claims he had already jumped, he just didn't know the amount.

Bellows had come up into the mountains to kill McCart, robbing gold mines was just an added benefit. "We're in Hickey, with the conditions that nobody commands my men except me, and only I am to kill McCart. You and your men are to stay away from him."

"What if he comes after us? It's almost certain he knows about me and my gang now, and that it was us who tried to kill him."

"That's different, if you kill him defending yourselves I'll understand. But don't go hunting him. Besides, as you have already found out, he isn't that easy to kill." They stood and shook hands, all the while each thinking about when he would kill the other. "Hickey, tell me more about the mines."

"There are three large mining operations. The Parrish mine is the largest, and holds more cash on hand than any of the others, but it also has the most men and guards. I planned on hitting it last, and then leaving the territory. The other two are the Youngblood and Walker mines. We were caught in a crossfire at the Youngblood mine the other day by surprise. They were not nearly as prepared when we scouted them a few days earlier. Someone has helped them improve their defenses. I believe it was this McCart fellow, who is now sheriff of Tin Cup."

"I have to agree. McCart was a Major in the Union Army, and I have it on good authority that he developed the strategies that helped General Ratcliff defeat the South at Gettysburg. If he is involved in helping the miners, I am going to have to scout these mines for myself."

"The two of us will ride out tomorrow and get a good look at these new defenses."

The next morning, Hickey and Bellows were ready to ride out when Bellows issued orders to his men. "Colton, you and Tate stay here with Hickey's men. Jasper, you ride back into Tin Cup and see if you can get eyes on the sheriff. Try to find out where he hails from and if it's McCart."

"You got it Boss."

"Hickey do you have a pair of moccasins?"

"No, why?"

"Colton, your his size, give him yours. You will need to put those on if you expect to get close enough to the mines without being heard."

While Hickey was putting on the moccasins he whispered to Marsh, "Don't go near our current stash, and whatever you do don't mention it to Bellows men. Make sure the others do the same."

Jasper stopped off at the general store first. Browsing around like he was looking for something to buy, he listened to the conversations going on within the store. Nothing was ever said about the sheriff, so he stepped up to the counter. "I'll take a pouch of that there tobacco and some papers." The clerk turned to grab the makings off the shelf behind him. "Here tell you all got a new sheriff in town. What's his name, could be I might know him?"

"His name is Mr. Hayes."

"No, doesn't sound familiar, do you happen to know where is he from?"

"I don't know, he keeps to himself pretty much, and he isn't much of a talker. All I know is he came up to hunt elk. That will be two bits sir. Is there anything else I can help you with?"

"No, that will be all, thanks."

Just as Jasper was walking out of the store, Randy was riding into town and saw him. Recognizing him as one of the men that had rode into the ranch with Quentin Bellows, Randy quickly rode behind the livery and out of site. Jasper walked down to Mabel's cafe hoping to get some more information. After he was seated, Mabel came up with a pot of coffee and greeted him. "Good morning, can I interest you in a plate of steak and eggs?"

Jasper couldn't remember the last time he had had sat down for a fresh cooked meal. "Sounds great." Mabel returned about ten minutes later with Jasper's breakfast. Jasper pulled his arms off the table to let Mabel put the plate in front of him. "I understand you have a new sheriff, the store owner said his name is Mr. Hayes. You wouldn't know where he is from would you?. I think I might know him, and I wouldn't want to leave town without saying hello."

"I understand he came from somewhere in Kansas."

Jasper knew enough to lie about knowing McCart. "No, can't rightly say I know anyone from Kansas. Thanks all the same."

"Enjoy your breakfast, and if I can be of any more help just give a yell."

Randy put his horse and mule into the livery's corral, and unsaddled them while he was thinking about what to do next. He didn't know where

Bellows and the others were, and he couldn't confront them alone. Grabbing his shotgun he walked over to the corner of the barn and peeked around to look down the street. He hadn't seen where the man had gone after leaving the store, so he had to wait until it was safe to show himself.

Logan was just walking out of his cabin when he saw Randy ride behind the livery. Wanting to surprise him he decided to sneak up from behind. Randy was so intent on watching the street, he hadn't heard Logan come up from behind. Logan shouted, "Hey! What are you hiding for?"

Randy jumped and uncontrollably pulled the trigger on his shotgun. The blast went off harmlessly into the dirt, but the whole town heard it, and everyone started running out into the street to see who was shooting. Nobody saw Jasper mount up and ride out of town during all the commotion.

Randy turned around. "Dammit Logan, what is it with you always scaring people?"

"The better question is, what are you doing here, and why are you skulking around?"

"I came to warn you. Bellows brother broke out of prison, and he is on his way here to kill you. I saw one of his men come out of the general store when I rode in, but I've lost sight of him."

Logan stepped out from behind the barn, "It's okay folks, there's nothing to be concerned about, go on about your business. Randy, lets walk around town and see if we can find this man."

After searching the tow, and not finding Jasper, they went to Mabel's for breakfast.

Randy recounted the story of Bellows and his men riding into the ranch wanting to kill him and his sister.

"I thought all that was behind us. I didn't even know Bellows had a brother."

"He was serving a life term in a Federal Prison in Missouri for murder. Logan, this man is more dangerous than his brother James. It's said he's lightning quick with a gun. He wasn't even concerned when Joey and your sister had the drop on him. It wasn't until I came up from behind them and pulled both the triggers back on my Greener that he gave up the fight. He vowed to return after killing you."

"How did he know where to find me?"

"Joey let it slip out that you were up here on a hunting trip. Don't blame him though Logan, he was willing to die for you and your sister."

"It's fine Randy, I'm sure Bellows would have found me one way or the other. I'm glad to hear Pearl's and my faith in Joey was well founded."

"Bellows wasn't none to happy to see Joey was working for you." Randy ate like he hadn't eaten for a week. "Logan, what is that star pinned to your chest?"

"I am the sheriff of Tin Cup. It's a long story. I'll fill you in when we get back to my cabin. You can stay with me until my business up here is finished. In the meantime, I got a couple friends I want you to meet. We'll ride over there tomorrow."

Randy and Logan rode up to the tree line and Logan hailed the mine. Charlie was standing guard. "Logan, great to see you son, get yourself in here. Who is that with you?"

"This is my guardian angel. Charlie, Gideon, I'd like you to meet Randy. He was nice enough to bring us another mule."

"Howdy Randy, any friend of Logan's is a friend of ours."

"Thanks, and I agree. This is some setup y'all got here."

"We have Logan to thank for that. He taught us how to build all this, not to mention the work he put in himself. Logan, have you told him how rich this mine has made you?"

Logan looked around sheepishly. It was Randy who responded, "What do you mean made him rich? Don't you two know, Logan is already a millionaire."

Bewildered, Charlie and Gideon looked at each other. "Why didn't you tell us Logan?"

"It's not something I like to talk about."

"Don't make no difference, your still an equal partner of the mine. You staked us, and did more than half the work around here."

That night they all sat around the camp fire, with Charlie and Gideon telling the story about how they all hooked up with Logan. Logan impressed upon Randy how important it was to keep the mine's existence secret, as well as keeping quiet about Charlie and Gideon being in the area to protect them from Hickey.

"Logan, what are you goin' to do if Bellows has hooked up with Hickey?"

"I don't know Charlie, but it might actually work to my favor."

"How's that?"

"If they join forces I won't have to be looking two different directions from which to be attacked. I am certain Bellows won't let Hickey interfere with his wanting to kill me himself."

"You have a point there." Not knowing Logan's history with overcoming great odds, Charlie asked, "But how are you goin' to handle nine men at once?"

"I will take the fight to them, and not wait for them to come after me."

Bellows and Hickey returned around dusk. Jasper had arrived just minutes earlier. Bellows walked over to the stove and filled his plate with stew. "Jasper, what did you learn about the sheriff?"

"There's no question about it Boss. He's using the name Hayes, but he fits the description for sure. The lady that owns the cafe said he came up from Kansas."

"That makes sense. Hayes is the same name he used in New York when he killed Ben Stiles for going after his sister. Did you get a look at him?"

"Sure did, seems there was some trouble down at the livery. I saw him when he stepped out to calm down the residents."

"Did he see you?"

"I don't think so, I rode out during all the commotion. The other boys told me you rode out to scout the mines. Did you learn anything useful?"

"I did Jasper. I am certain McCart helped the miners set up their defenses. But he made one mistake. They all have the same defense. Each mine has a man posted outside the perimeter to sound the alarm, and the compounds are all protected by four or more men to catch any attackers in a crossfire."

"That doesn't sound like much of a mistake to me."

"The mistake is that they all have the same vulnerability."

"What's that?"

"Once we take out the lookout, we can circle around and take out the perimeter guards. Then we will be able to overpower the remaining guards with our superior force."

Hickey approved of the plan. He would let Bellows and his men take the lead. With any luck, his men would be able to kill Bellows and his men during the Parrish raid, which is scheduled for last. However, he was still concerned about McCart. "What about the sheriff Bellows, he isn't going to just set back in town while we are raiding the mines. After we hit the Walker mine he will be coming after us for sure. When are you going after him?"

"I'm not, as you said he will come after us, and when he does I will have a trap set for him."

"What kind of trap?"

"That's my problem, you don't have to concern yourself with my killing him."

Hickey was beginning to think Bellows might be setting a trap for him and his men as well. Just like he was planning a trap for them.

Chapter 23

Logan and Randy had returned to town. As he made his usual rounds, Logan introduced Randy to the merchants and Dan Clady. Randy only had one job. Keep his eyes peeled for Bellows men.

Eight men mounted up to raid the Walker mine. "Jasper, I want you to go back to Tin Cup. Here, take my field glasses. Don't enter the town, find a place up on the ridge and keep an eye on the sheriff. I want to know what he's doing and who he's talking to. If he leaves town I want you to follow him, make sure he doesn't see you."

When the gang was about a half mile south of the Walker mine they pulled up. "Colton, you and Tate are the only two wearing moccasins. Slip up there and take out the lookout. Kill him with your knife, I don't want any shots fired. The rest of you dismount, we'll wait here until they return."

An hour had passed when Colton and Tate returned. "He's dead Boss."

"Good job Colton. Now, lets circle around on foot and take out those perimeter guards. Tate you stay here with the horses. When you hear the shooting bring them down to the compound, but don't ride in, stay hidden back in the tree line until I call for you."

The two perimeter guards put up a fight, but they were no match for the seven skilled gunfighters. There was only one guard outside the office. He quickly ran low on ammunition and gave up. He would soon learn that was a mistake. After telling them where the safe was, Hickey killed him and the clerk inside. As usual, Hickey wasn't going to leave any witnesses that could identify him. The safe was inferior and the hinges were easily broken with a crowbar and hammer. The take was twenty thousand in cash, and five thousand dollars worth of gold dust.

Knowing that the shots might have been heard throughout the mountains, the gang rode at a gallop back to the cabin. "Not much of a take to split up between eight men Hickey."

"I didn't expect much from the Walker mine. The Youngblood and Parrish mines will be far more lucrative. But you're welcome to pull out any time."

"You would like that wouldn't you. I think we'll stick around and see it through. But you better be right about the take from the other mines. How can you be sure they haven't been packing the gold down off the mountain?"

"We have been watching the only two routes out of the Pass. There hasn't been a single mule train leave the territory since we arrived. They have been selling their gold in Tin Cup and keeping the cash at the mines."

"Why not wait and rob the assay office when they transport it?"

"It's too well guarded, and we can't handle that much weight in raw gold and ore."

Hickey's men were huddled together outside the cabin. None of them liked the new arrangements. "Marsh, this isn't right, with these new men our shares are being reduced from twenty thousand each to just over ten thousand."

"I agree Spivey, but let's see what Hickey has planned before we act. I can't believe he is willing to share with Bellows."

They hadn't noticed Hickey walk up behind them. "What are you boys talking about?"

Marsh spoke for the group. "Boss, there won't be enough money to split between eight of us."

"I agree. It's my plan to kill Bellows and his men during the Parrish raid. Keep quiet and act as if nothing is wrong. Don't give them any reason to mistrust us."

The group discussion outside had not went unnoticed by Bellows. When Hickey walked back into the cabin, he asked, "What was the pow-wow outside all about?"

"Nothing, the men were talking about how pleased they were with how well things went at the Walker mine today."

"I doubt it will be so easy next time."

"They're seasoned men Quentin. They have been with me a long time and are up to the task."

"Let's hope so."

Jasper was laying down on top the ridge overlooking Tin Cup when the rider came galloping into town yelling. He couldn't make out the words, but was sure it had something to do with the raid on the Walker mine.

Logan came rushing out of the saloon with Randy right on his heels. As the horse came to a sliding halt on it's haunches, Logan reached up and took hold of the reins. The rider came flying out of the saddle still yelling. "Sheriff, they attacked and robbed the Walker mine."

"Who did?"

"I don't know, I stayed inside the mine with the others. They showered the mouth of the mine with lead, and we were to vulnerable to come out. Being well back from the opening we could only see their images. We counted seven men. They killed all the guards and the clerk inside the office."

Jasper kept a close eye on the happenings below. It didn't take long before Logan, Randy, Clady and Emmitt all rode out following the Walker miner. Jasper was surprised when he saw Randy fill up the field glasses. He knows Bellows instructed him to follow the sheriff, but felt Quentin would be more interested in knowing this man was in Tin Cup. Besides, it was obvious where the sheriff was headed.

Jasper raced up to the cabin. Bellows and Hickey came running out onto the porch. "Jasper, what's wrong?"

"You're not going to believe this Boss. You remember that old geezer that covered us with the shotgun at McCart's ranch?"

"Of course I do, what about him?"

"He's here. I saw him ride out of town with the sheriff."

Bellows wasn't all that surprised by the news that Randy was in Tin Cup. He thought it would have taken the ranch longer to get a man here to warn McCart. "I had the advantage with McCart not knowing about me. Now I'll have to change my plans. Thanks Jasper, you did the right thing by coming back. Take care of your horse and get yourself something to eat."

Logan and his men rode into the compound of the Walker mine. The other five miners were digging graves to bury the dead. One of the men walked over to the group of riders. "Sheriff, it all happened so fast. We didn't even get a warning."

"What happened to the lookout?"

"Somehow they knew he was there, and they cut his throat before he could get off a shot."

"Is Mr. Walker around?"

"He's dead. He was standing guard at the office when they attacked. He gave up and told them where the money was, then one of them just up and shot him for no reason, along with the clerk."

"What's your name and what is your position?"

"I'm called Stoney, and I'm the foreman."

"Stoney, can you describe the man that shot Walker and the clerk?"

"I didn't see him, but Eddy, the clerk in the office, lived long enough to say the man that shot them had blonde hair and blue eyes."

"That was Hickey."

While the men completed the burials, Logan searched the outskirts of the compound. He found where Hickey's men had circled around and got behind the perimeter guards. The guards didn't have a chance. Logan was familiar with Hickey's tactics, and this wasn't his work. Based upon the numbers, and having found moccasin tracks up where the lookout was killed, Logan was convinced Hickey and Bellows had joined forces. He had to get word about the raid to the Youngblood and Parrish mines.

"Stoney, did Walker have any relatives or partners?"

"No living relatives that I am aware of, his parents passed on a couple years ago. As far as the ownership of the mine goes, Mr. Walker held fifty-one percent. The remaining seven of us, sorry, make that six now, each have an equal share of the remaining forty-nine percent."

"It is too dangerous to continue operations right now Stoney. Gather the men, I want to talk to them." Stoney did as the sheriff requested.

"Men, my name is Logan Hayes, also known as Logan McCart."

A couple of the men recognized the name McCart, and one of them shouted out, "You that same McCart what took on the Bellows gang down in Kansas?"

"Yes. Men, I can't promise you anything, but I will do my best to get your money back. In the meantime I am asking for volunteers."

"You looking for a posse to go after those varmints?"

"No posse, I will be going after them myself. But I am looking for men to help guard the Youngblood mine."

"What's in it for us, we don't have any interest in that mine."

"I will pay each man that volunteers a thousand dollars. If I retrieve your stolen money and gold you will reimburse me. If I don't, the thousand dollars is yours to keep."

It was Stoney that asked, "How long are we talking about? I want to get back here to continue operations. We have a good claim here, and there's no reason to give it up."

"Until I capture the Hickey gang, or I am killed. Either way, I don't expect it to be more than a month at most. I am riding out in five minutes, you have until then to decide."

After a heated discussion Stoney looked back over at Logan. "When do we get the thousand dollars?"

"I will have the assay office wire for the money when I get back to town. I should be able to issue a draft against it within a few days."

All right mister, you got yourself six new guards."

Pleased that the miners were willing to help protect the other mine, Logan turned his attention back to Clady. "Dan, you and Emmitt ride over to the Parrish mine. Tell them what happened here, and advise them to double their guard. I will take these men over to the Youngblood mine. One more thing Dan, have Parrish move his lookout back into the compound. Now that Hickey knows they are out there, they will be in too much danger."

Logan rode into the courtyard of the Youngblood mine with the six new volunteers. Mr. Youngblood met them out on the porch, which has been fortified per Logan's earlier instructions. Logan told him of the raid on the Walker mine, and that the men behind him had volunteered to help guard his mine.

Mr. Youngblood was being his stubborn self. "You are pretty free about enlarging my payroll Logan."

"These men are being paid by me, and it will not cost you an extra penny for the added protection."

Mr. Youngblood was once again surprised. "Logan, I could use a man with your integrity and intelligence. Why don't you come to work for me full time? I promise you will make ten times more than you are earning as sheriff."

"Thanks, but I accepted the job, and I'll see it through. Double your perimeter guard, use two additional men to watch the backs of the outside perimeter guards while they watch the compound. Take your lookout and post him inside the office."

"Very well, I'll do as you suggest. You haven't been wrong yet."

Having done all he could for the moment, Logan and Randy headed back to town. "Randy, ride over to Mabel's and order us supper. I will be over in a few minutes." Logan went over to the assay office, which also doubled as a bank. He sent a draft to the Kansas State Bank for six thousand dollars. Four days later the authorization to draw down against the draft was received by the assay office. It helped that the Assay office sent a rider to Salida every day. The army had established a small outpost there and set up a telegraph wire.

Things had been quiet so he rode out to pay the volunteers. When he rode in one of the office clerks went to get Stoney. "Glad to see you McCart, my men were getting concerned about whether or not you were going to honor your word. They were wanting to head back to our own mine, but I told them they could trust you. Any progress on finding Hickey?"

"I know where he is, I'll be going after them in another day or so. You just keep your men focused and alert. I am sure Hickey will make another play sometime soon."

"Look, I heard the stories and I know you like to work alone. But are you sure you don't want us to ride with you?"

"Thanks Stoney, but these are skilled gunfighters, and I don't want any of you killed going up against them."

Logan spent the next day and a half preparing to go after Hickey and Bellows. He thought about riding Blue, because he wouldn't stand out against the terrain as much as Dusty. But after careful consideration he finally decided on Dusty. Mostly because he was war tested, and less likely to spook or run away at the sound of gunfire. After saddling Dusty he turned his attention to Sallie and packed what supplies he thought he might need for a couple days.

"Randy, I should be back in about a week. If I'm not back you know what to do."

"I know, get a message off to Brodie."

"Good. Keep your head down and don't get into any trouble."

James "Pearl" Brodie is a U.S. Federal Marshall living in Lawrence, Kansas, and a good friend of Logan's. He would come running, and take care of Hickey and Bellows if anything happened to Logan.

After making one last check of his weapons, he rode out to get Hickey and Bellows, or die trying.

Randy watched Logan ride out. He knows how dangerous these men are, but he also knows how dangerous Logan can be when tracking down those who have wronged him. He also knew Logan would not quit until he has either killed them, or he was dead himself. Randy prayed for his safe return.

Chapter 24

Hickey and Bellows spent the last couple of days preparing to hit the Youngblood mine again. "Bellows, have you given any more thought to killing McCart?"

"That is all I have been thinking about. In fact, I am going to use this raid to set a trap for him, and you are going to help."

"Are you crazy, it is going to take every man we have to take that mine. You saw as well as I did that they have doubled the guard. This ain't going to be a walk in the park like the Walker job."

"I realize that, that is why we aren't going to take the Youngblood mine tomorrow."

"Then what are we going there for, a picnic?"

"You and your men are going to mount an assault as we planned, but you are only going to make it appear you are trying to rob the mine."

"What's the purpose of that?"

"Jasper has informed me that McCart is preparing to come after us. While you are mounting an attack on the mine, me and my men will be spread out up above to surround him when he comes to help."

"I don't like this Bellows, you are placing me and my men in danger just to satisfy your own personal vendetta."

"Well, like you said to me, you can pull out anytime. But the Walker loot stays with me. Or maybe you think you can kill me, and keep it all for yourself?"

Hickey was fast and a stone cold killer, but he didn't like the situation. "I am up here to get rich, and I ain't leaving until I am. We will do our part tomorrow, just make sure you do yours so we can get back to the business at hand, and clear out of here. It won't take much more killing and the army will come in to maintain order."

"Tate, saddle up, we are going to scout the hills above the mine." There were only two direct routes leading into the mine. One where the hills funneled down into a draw leading directly into the compound from the south, and another where the land flattened out for about fifty yards behind the mine that was protected by the perimeter guards. The office backed up against the east side of the mountain, and of course the mine was dug straight into the mountain face on the north side. There was no possible approach by horse from either of those two directions. It was unlikely a man could enter from either of those directions without the use of a rope and exposing himself.

Since the lookout had been moved back inside the compound, Bellows and Tate had no problem approaching the hills outside the mine unnoticed. "Tate, find yourself a high spot where you can cover both the south and west openings. If Logan tries coming over the top of the mountain from the east or north, I'll take care of him when he exposes himself."

Tate returned not long after finding his spot for the ambush. "Boss, I found the perfect spot where I can cover both directions. What do you want me to do after I shoot McCart?"

"I want you to kill Hickey and his men."

"Won't we need them later to help rob the mine?"

"No, while you and the perimeter guards are fighting Hickey. Me and the other boys will slip in and steal the cash. We won't be coming back later."

"What about the Parrish mine?"

"They have too many men. Besides, Colton has learned that Hickey has another sixty thousand stashed back at the cabin. That, along with the seventy-five thousand Hickey says is down there we'll have plenty. Then we will ride to Mexico."

Not trusting Bellows, Hickey gathered his men up at the mine behind the cabin. "Porter, tomorrow after we start the attack I want you to slip away. and find Tate, and kill him. He is Bellows best sharpshooter, and will be strategically placed to ambush both McCart and us."

"But Boss, he's on our side."

"Maybe, but I believe Bellows is going to include us in his trap. If I am wrong we'll just say the guards killed him. If I am right, Tate will have us in a crossfire between himself and the guards. If that happens I want everyone to break off the fight and circle back to the horses. We will meet back at the mine. Don't approach the cabin. We will figure out how to take care of Bellows and the other two men tonight."

Bellows and Tate rode in just as Hickey and his men were breaking up. "What was all that about Hickey? You and your men always seem to be holding secret meetings."

"I was just going over the attack plan with my men. Are you all set up?"

"Yeah, don't forget, keep up the attack until one of my men lets you know we got McCart." Nothing else was said. The tension was high between the two groups with each not trusting the other.

Logan had been watching the cabin when Bellows and Tate came riding up. Logan recognized Bellows from the description Randy had given him, the resemblance to his brother was. striking. He was too far away to hear any of the conversations, but he could tell by their body language that Hickey and Bellows weren't too friendly toward each other. All the same, it was clear that they had joined forces and were planning something.

Slipping back down over the rise to my horses, I settled in for a cold camp that night. I sure missed my coffee, but I had to stay close and keep my movements hidden.

The next morning everyone down at the cabin was busy saddling their horses, and they were armed to the teeth. There was no doubt they were going to hit one of the mines, but which one. If I ride to warn the wrong mine I will be of no help. I have no choice but to follow them. After they rode out I tied Sallie to a tree. She would not be able to keep pace, and could alert the killers to my presence by following. There was no need to remain close. Eight horses would not be that difficult to track. Besides, the mines were well enough protected to hold off any attack until I could move up and join the fight.

The night before, Bellows had filled in Jasper and Colton of his plans to kill Hickey and his men, and how they would rob the mine while the guards were occupied by Hickey's gang. None of the men were talking as they rode, but they all kept a close eye on one another. The gang tethered their horses well back and out of sight of the mine.

"Hickey, we'll wait here for McCart. You take your men and set up for the attack. Wait fifteen minutes then open fire."

"What do you plan on doing during that time?"

"I am going to set my trap for McCart. If I am right he has been following us. Now get moving, and don't stop firing until Colton comes and gives you the all clear."

I wasn't more than a couple minutes away from the mine when I heard the gun fire echo through the mountains. Not wanting to ride straight into the bandits, I swung south to come in behind them. I was approaching slowly as I tried to determine where the attack was being concentrated. Focused on the attack, I wasn't paying attention to anything else around me, and that's when a Grizzly appeared out of the trees and spooked Dusty, causing him to turn sharply to the side. The bullet smacked the tree just behind where I would have been if Dusty had not leapt to the side. Spurring Dusty hard, I rode into a small group of rocks, where I dove off my horse for cover just as the second bullet ricocheted off the rocks.

Tate wasn't sure if he had hit McCart with his second shot or not. He questioned himself as to whether he should check to make sure Logan was dead, or turn and take the fight to Hickey. He decided it was too dangerous to risk turning his back to McCart. If he is still alive, he is to dangerous to be left behind and allowed to stalk him. Tate had to make sure McCart is dead before turning his attention to Hickey. Besides, Hickey and his men would keep up the attack until Colton came to tell them it was clear. Knowing Colton wasn't coming to warn them, he felt Hickey would remain engaged with the guards until he could finish off McCart.

After hearing the shots from Tate's position, Bellows led Jasper and Colton down to the mine. They remained on foot, and stayed under cover of the tree line while they crept up along the side of the office unnoticed. The guards on the office porch focused their attention on the battle across the compound, and were unaware of Bellows and his men approaching from behind. After shooting the porch guards, Bellows stepped into the office to find it empty. Taking Logan's advice, Youngblood had moved the safe into the mine itself in case the guards were overrun. Bellows cursed, "Dammit, this is McCart's doing. Let's get out of here."

Tate was well concealed, so he maintained his position and kept a close eye on the rocks where McCart had disappeared. Logan was protected by the rocks, but there was nowhere to move that wouldn't place him out in the open. He decided to wait until after sunset before going after his bushwhacker.

Hickey heard the gunshots coming from across the compound. Looking up he saw Bellows enter the office. When Bellows came right back out without any money bags. It was obvious his attempt to cross him had failed. Hickey turned to his men, "Get to the horses."

They had already lost Dillon on the last raid, and Marsh didn't want to lose any more men. "Boss what about Porter, he's out there all alone?"

"Don't worry about Porter, he will meet us back at the mine."

Logan had been lying still for more than an hour when he heard the report of the Sharps, but no bullet hit near the rocks protecting him. It dawned on him that the shots taken at him earlier had come from a Henry rifle. The man that fired the Sharps had to be the same man that had bushwhacked him up in the pass, and Youngblood's men just out of town. That meant Hickey's and Bellows' men were turning on each other.

The bullet smashed into Tate's back. Splitting his spine, and allowing him to live just long enough to understand he had been shot from behind. Porter came up to verify his kill. Complimenting himself on his skilled shot, he looked in the same direction that Tate had been watching. If McCart was down there he couldn't see him. It would be dark shortly, and his advantage with the Sharps would be gone. Knowing McCart's uncanny ability to stay alive, Porter didn't believe he was dead. The gunfire below had stopped. Porter retreated, and after finding his horse alone where they had left them, he rode back to the mine.

Keeping his voice low, Porter softly hailed the mine. Hickey was standing just inside the shaft. "Come on in Porter."

"Tate's dead Boss. You were right about the double cross."

"What about McCart, is he dead?"

"Tate was keeping watch over a stand of rocks, so I don't think he killed McCart. That's why he hadn't turned to brace us."

"Who killed Tate, you or McCart?"

"I did."

"Good, as far as Bellows knows we don't know anything about his plan to kill us. We will tell him McCart killed Tate."

"Boss we can't attack the mines and protect ourselves against Bellows men at the same time."

"We aren't going to Spivey. The mines are too well protected now. We are going to cut ties with Bellows and rob the assay office."

Hickey and his men backtracked and rode up to the cabin from the west. He wanted it to appear they were returning from the Youngblood mine. Stepping out onto the porch Bellows challenged him. "Where the hell have you been?"

"We were waiting for Colton and the all clear, what happened?"

"The miners flushed us out. There were to many of them so we had to cut and run." Of course Hickey knew he was lying, but Bellows didn't know that. "Did you see my man Tate?"

Hickey let a smile drift across his face. "He's dead. We found him face down with a bullet in his back. Guess McCart is not ready to die just yet."

Bellows wanted to kill Hickey right on the spot to wipe that smile off his face. He lowered his hand to his pistol and realized the hammer thong was still hooked. Looking at Hickey he noticed his pistol was free. The advantage was Hickey's. "Step down and we'll go inside to make plans for our next raid."

"No, there is too much resistance now. My boys and I are clearing out. We'll stay up at the mine tonight and ride out tomorrow morning."

Bellows wasn't happy with the turn of events. If Hickey wanted to spend the night up at the mine, then he knows about the double cross. It also meant his stash was hidden up in the mine. He had no choice but to wait and kill him later. Right now he had to return to his first priority, which is killing McCart. "Fine, have it your way, I'll see you in the morning before you leave."

Chapter 25

It was well after sunset by the time Logan had worked his way up the ridge and found Tate. Striking a Lucifer, he turned the dead man over to get a look at his face. He didn't recognize the man, meaning he was most likely part of Bellows gang. One thing was for sure, that hole in his back was made from a 54 caliber Sharps. No gun fire had come from inside the mineshaft. That meant Youngblood and his money were still safe.

Logan had made the recommendation to move the safe into the mine outside the hearing of everyone except Mr. Youngblood. He and his two most trusted men were the only ones, except Logan, that knew about the safe being moved inside the mine.

Not wanting to take the risk of crippling his horse, Logan walked back trailing Dusty behind him. Reaching his camp, he gathered up Sallie and took both animals down to the creek for a much needed drink. Sallie appeared undisturbed, and there were no tracks to indicate anyone had found her.

I crawled up to the top of the ridge on my belly to see what was happening down at the cabin. I really wasn't surprised to see a camp fire up at the mine, and smoke coming out of the chimney from the cabin. They had split up, neither trusting the other enough to be in the same place. Sliding back down the hill I crawled under my saddle blanket and went to sleep.

It's doubtful that either group would attack the mines on their own. While that was a good development, it will make it more difficult for Logan to arrest them if they split up. Somehow he needed to find out what they were planning. That morning Logan crept up to within fifty feet of the cabin when Hickey and his men came riding down from the mine. They were riding with their rifles at the ready in case Bellows wanted to start any trouble.

Seeing Hickey and his group coming down from the mine, Bellows had stepped out onto the porch. He could see the swell in Hickey's saddlebags, but those rifles pointed in his direction weren't for show. He had no choice but to let Hickey and his men ride out with the money. "That's it then, your going to call it quits and leave all that money behind?"

"That money isn't any good to us if we're dead. The miners are too well fortified thanks to your Mr. McCart."

Bellows men had moved to the windows, and were covering Hickey's gang with their rifles. It would only take one man to make a mistake and all hell would break loose. Although his men were under cover, Bellows was out in the open and sure to be shot. "Ride out Hickey, and don't let me see you again, or I will kill you."

Now it was Hickey who wanted to kill Bellows on the spot. However, with Bellows men inside the cabin under cover, they had the advantage. Hickey spurred his horse and rode past Bellows without taking his eyes or rifle off him.

Watching Hickey's gang ride away, Logan started to turn and crawl back to his camp when the bullet threw dirt up into his face. Bellows sprang for cover as Jasper was yelling at him. "Boss, McCart's out there in the trees."

"Did you get him?"

"I don't think so."

"Grab my rifle and get out here. We're going after him."

I was so intent on trying to hear what Bellows and Hickey were saying I had raised up and given myself away. Scrambling back on my hands and knees to my horses, I heard the rifle crack as the bullet splintered the tree next to my face. There was no time to get mounted and ride out. All I could do was cut the picket lines to free the horses. I ran down to the creek as fast as my legs would carry me. Darting in between the trees to protect my back.

Out numbered, my only advantage was the terrain, and hoping I knew the countryside better than my pursuers. I was glad I had taken the opportunity to scout this area before heading north to hunt. Running up the other side of the creek, I ducked into a tight crevice just as a volley of bullets hit all around me. The crevice was just wide enough for a man to squeeze into, and it ran all the way through to the other side of the hill. I would never have entered it otherwise. It was three against one, and I couldn't allow myself to be trapped in a cave.

Bellows was visibly upset with McCart having eluded them. But he took comfort in the fact that he thought McCart was trapped. "We have him now boys. All we have to do is wait him out. He can't stay in there forever. His supplies are on his mule, and he doesn't have any food or water. Colton, slip back up to the cabin and grab us a couple of canteens and some jerky."

Logan was crawling up to the top of the hill on the other side of the cave when he heard Bellows give Colton his orders. Sliding back down the hill he ran around it, bringing him out above the cabin. Seeing Colton go inside, he worked his way down to their horses where their canteens still hung off the saddles. It wasn't long before Colton came out and started towards the horses to retrieve the canteens.

I positioned myself behind the trees between the horses and the cabin. Colton set his rifle down, leaning it up against the corral poles, and reached up for the first canteen. As silently as possible I came up from behind him. Just as he was about to turn I covered his mouth with my hand, and using my knife I cut his throat all the way to the bone. Quietly I lowered Colton to the ground and reached to grab his rifle.

Colton had been gone too long, and Bellows sent Jasper back to see what was holding him up. As Jasper came up to the cabin he saw Logan reaching for the rifle and he snapped off a quick shot. By not taking the time to aim, his shot was off target and hit Logan in the leg instead of the chest. Logan limped off toward the mine as Jasper snapped off a couple more quick shots. Again his shots were to hurried to hit anything.

Bellows came running back. "Jasper, what happened, where's Colton?"

"McCart killed him. I shot him in the leg and he ran into the mine shaft."

"I don't know how he got out of that cave, but he ain't getting out of that mine. Go up to the cabin and get me a couple sticks of dynamite."

Logan was losing blood from his wound. Cutting a piece off his shirt tail he plugged the exit wound. After emptying two of the cylinders of his pistol, he poured the powder of the combustible cartridges into the entry hole in his thigh. Then he struck a Lucifer and placed it on top the entry wound, flashing the gunpowder to cauterize the wound and stop the bleeding. Then wrapped his leg with his neckerchief. Fortunately the bullet didn't strike the bone.

Aside from a limp, Logan could still walk. Finding an oil lamp, he fired it up and moved farther back into the mine. It was pitch dark and the light didn't penetrate very far. He was walking back to the mouth of the mine when the dynamite sticks landed just inside the entrance. Seeing the burning fuse he turned to run to the back of the shaft. The blast caused the mine entrance to collapse, trapping him inside.

Bellows was laughing. "He won't dig his way out of that. If the blast didn't kill him, he will suffocate by morning. We will stay here tonight and make sure he doesn't dig himself out."

"What then Boss?"

"Then we go after Hickey. He has approximately sixty thousand dollars in his saddle bags."

Logan had been knocked out by the concussion blast from the dynamite. It was pitch dark and he was covered in dust. His head was pounding from the concussion of the blast.

I slowly regained my senses. The air was still filled with dust. Yet aside from that, I wasn't having as much trouble breathing as I would have thought. Rolling over onto my side I felt the sharp pain in my leg. With my head pounding as it was, I had forgotten all about being shot in the leg. My neckerchief was still wrapped around the leg, and fortunately the blast had not reopened the wound. With the wound still closed, I untied the neckerchief from my leg and wrapped it around my face to reduce the dust I was breathing in. Feeling along the floor of the mine I found the kerosene lantern. The blast must have blown out the wick. Lighting the lamp I moved to the mine opening, or what used to be an opening. It was completely sealed and too much rock to move. Things were looking pretty bleak, and there didn't appear to be any way out of this predicament. This is the one thing I had tried to avoid, trapping myself in a cave. I sat down to conserve my energy while I thought of how I might escape. When I set the lantern down, I noticed the black smoke was being drawn off towards the back of the mine. Although I couldn't feel it, there had to be a draft drawing the smoke deeper into the mine. Grabbing the lantern I walked toward the back of the mine. It was probably just wishful thinking that there was another opening. It was more than likely that the smoke merely had nowhere else to go but further back into the mine. But the farther back I went, the fresher the air seemed to get. I couldn't see any light streaming into the mine. I hadn't realized how long I had been knocked out and that it was night time. Just before reaching out to touch the back wall of the mine, my foot hit what appeared to be a large rock. Lowering the lamp to get a closer look I saw it wasn't a rock, but instead a ledge that had been chiseled out. It was large enough for a man to stand or sit on, and there was a bucket filled with water. After washing out my mouth and eyes I sat down and drank from the gourd hanging over the bucket. Weak from the bullet wound in my leg, and still recovering from the blast, I needed rest and regain my strength. Blowing out the lamp I sat down on the ledge and leaned back, and drifted off to sleep.

When I woke up, a stream of light was irritating my eyes. I cursed myself for leaving the lamp lit and wasting the kerosene. While admonishing myself, I remembered specifically blowing out the lamp before setting it down. Looking up I saw a faint bit of light streaming past a large rock. Standing up I positioned myself over to the side to get a better look at where the light was streaming through. When I touched the wall to brace myself, I felt a small indentation cut out of the wall. Straining my eyes and feeling higher up the wall, I realized there was a number of toe and hand holds leading up to the top of the shaft. Lighting the lamp I held it up above my head. The blast had apparently caused a huge rock outside to shift and cover a sizable opening. Logan caught himself speaking out loud, "Thank you Benny." Two Time Benny was an experienced miner, and as such, he always built an escape route against a cave-in.

Using the foot holes, I climbed up to the top of the shaft. It was no use, as hard as I tried, I couldn't budge the rock. It was too heavy, and it wasn't going to move no matter how hard I pushed. The climb had taken all my strength, and once again I found myself fatigued. After a short rest and drink of water I went to the front of the mine. I was looking for anything I could use to pry the rock out. The blast tore out several logs that had been used for bracing. But they were to short to reach the boulder. I found a pick and hammer which might allow me to break the rock. Using the ripped out logs, I was able to build a stairway by bracing the logs an at angle against the shaft walls. Crisscrossing them as I worked my way up to the top. Not the best ladder I ever made, but it would support me, and allow my hands to be free to work on that rock.

After a couple of hours of chipping away at the edges of the rock, I got it to move. Using the pick I pushed up on the side that showed the most movement. Pushing with all my might I was able to lift the rock slightly, but I was too weak to roll it out of the way. Exhausted from all the work over the last couple of hours, I climbed down to rest and quench my thirst. I drank sparingly not knowing how long I might be trapped.

The pick wasn't heavy enough, or long enough, to give me the leverage I needed to roll the boulder out of the way. Searching around I found a six foot long brace about eight inches round. Placing one end against the rock, and my hands underneath the other end, I pushed with my legs and back. The rock moved, but still not enough. With my remaining strength, I put everything I had into it with my entire body. The rock started to roll over, and sensing I wouldn't have another chance, I heaved with all my energy. The rock turned up and over. It wasn't fully clear, but with a little prying, I was able to move the boulder off to the side. I had moved the boulder enough to allow me to squeeze pass.

Using my legs that hard had started the bleeding again, but not enough to be concerned. The escape shaft came out directly above the cabin. Laying on my stomach and catching my breath, I watched the cabin for any signs of life. The horses were gone and there wasn't any sign of Bellows or Jasper. Standing up I walked down to the cabin. Everyone and their belongings were gone, and there was no sign they would be returning. Covered in dirt I walked down to the creek. There was no need to undress, so I went in clothes and all to wash away the dirt and sweat that was clinging to me and my clothes. I was filling my throat with water when I heard the horse. Rolling over I drew my pistol. It was Dusty, Sallie came in about five minutes later. Tightening the cinch I mounted up and headed back to town.

As I rode into Tin Cup I could tell something was wrong. The towns folk were all coming out of there places of business. They were looking straight at me, and with some mighty unfriendly looks, murmuring as if I was the enemy. I searched the crowd, but didn't see Randy among them. As I was unsaddling Dusty and Sallie at the cabin, Clady came up to the corral.

Clady could see Logan had been shot, and looked pretty ragged and worn out. "You alright Sheriff?"

"I'll be fine. What has the town folk all riled up? They didn't seem to friendly as I rode in."

"The assay office was robbed last night. They lost their life savings."

"And what, they think I did it?"

"No, but they blame you for it."

"Me, why?"

"The robbery happened last night. We can't be sure, but we think it was Hickey. The town people think you should have been here protecting them, and not out chasing ghosts, or helping the miners."

Logan pointed to his wounded leg. "Ghosts, you think ghosts did this?"

"Relax Logan, I'm on your side, but there is something else. A man named Bellows came riding in this morning and braced Randy. Acted like he knew him and gloated about killing you. That is when Randy got mad and shot Bellows partner with his shotgun. Bellows shot Randy before he could turn the shotgun on him."

"Is Randy dead?"

"He is over at Doc's, but it doesn't look good."

"What direction did Bellows go?"

"He hasn't left, he is still over at the saloon drinking."

Logan pulled his revolver and checked the loads. After replacing the two empty cylinders he pushed Clady aside and started toward the saloon. Stepping inside he saw Bellows sitting at a table toward the back. "Stand up Bellows, this ends here."

"I'll be damned. If you aren't the toughest man I ever did kill. How did you survive that mine blast?"

"Turns out Benny built an escape tunnel. Being an experienced miner he always wanted a way out in case of a cave-in."

"My younger brother was the best when it came to knife fighting. I don't know how you bested him, but I am going to fill you full of lead. You must think your a fast man with that gun to walk in here and brace me all alone."

"You are going to find out real soon. Now stand up and draw."

Bellows' hate for this man was filling his throat. "I am going to kill you for killing my brother, just like you killed him for murdering your parents."

"Your brother was a stinking skunk, just like you."

Bellows drew while he was standing up out of the chair. Both men were now firing. Bellows' shots were going wild as Logan's bullets pounded into his chest. Logan's pistol was now empty, but he was still pulling the trigger, with the hammer falling on empty chambers.

Clady came up from behind Logan and wrapped his arms around his chest and arms. "It's over Logan, he is dead."

Logan cleared his eyes from all the smoke, and looked down at the lifeless body. Bellows had six bullets holes surrounding his heart.

Logan stepped into the doctor's office. Randy looked up and a broad smile crossed his face seeing Logan alive. "That was some ruckus I heard down at the saloon. Did you kill him?"

"He is burning in hell with his brother. I thought you had cashed in your chips old man."

"I may not be as tough as you, but I don't die that easy. Logan, I found the tracks from the assay office robbery. Hickey and his men are headed southwest. They are headed straight toward Charlie and Gideon. Odds are they will find the mine."

Logan turned around and was facing Clady. "Dan, tell the town's people they will get their money back" With that said, Logan walked out and headed back to his cabin.

Randy was still in danger of dying. He had put on a brave face in front of Logan because he knew Charlie and Gideon were in serious danger, and that only Logan could save them. If Logan had known how serious Randy's wounds were, he might not have left to help them.

There was no time to waste. Dusty was tired from the hard and fast ride back, so Logan saddled up Blue. He slid his Hawken into the rifle boot and carried his Henry repeater over his saddle as he rode out. His LeMat hung over the saddle horn.

Chapter 26

Logan was about a mile out when he heard the gunfire and spurred Blue into a trot. Still well back in the trees he dismounted and tied Blue to a branch. Easing his way through the trees he saw Hickey and his men behind some rocks pumping lead into the entrance of the mine.

Charlie and Gideon were well protected behind the perimeter wall. They were shooting back, but sparingly. Either they couldn't get a good shot, or they were low on ammunition. Knowing Charlie as he did, he figured it was the latter.

Logan decided to get into the game. He fired three quick shots at Hickey's position. All of a sudden everyone stopped firing.

"Boss, someone is shooting at us from that tree line."

Hickey snapped at Spivey. "I know that you idiot. It has to be either that McCart fellow, or Bellows."

"What do we do?"

"Porter, circle around and take him out." Porter gripped his Sharps and slid out through the back of the rocks. "Marsh, you and Spivey lay down some fire on that tree line and keep him busy until Porter can get around behind him."

"What about those two old timers up at the mine?"

"They aren't going to leave the cover of the mine, now do as your told."

Logan was trying to determine how many of men were down in the rocks. Two were now peppering his location, and one continued to fire at the mine. Although he could distinguish three different shooters, something was nagging at him. Then it hit him, he hadn't heard the Sharps since he had opened fire on them. Quickly Logan laid his rifle down and covered it with leaves. Slipping back to his horse, he pulled the Hawken out of the rifle boot and slung the saddle holster over his shoulder. Not only did the holster hold the LeMat. The pouch held the powder and lead shot for the Hawken. Lastly, Logan pulled his moccasins out of his saddle bags and disappeared into the woods on foot.

Every step was crucial now. Porter had proven himself an exceptional shot and adept at concealment. The first one to make a mistake would die. When Logan was well back into the woods, he sat down and switched out of his boots into his moccasins. Charlie and Gideon were well positioned and protected inside the mine. Hickey wasn't going to get to them any time soon. Logan had to turn all his focus to Porter if he was going to survive.

Porter was closing in on the spot where the man had been firing from the trees. Using his spy glass Porter surveyed the trees. Whoever it was he was gone now. Still not wanting to expose himself, Porter remained very still and quiet. He continued to look over the terrain with his spy glass. Then he heard the horse whinny. Returning the spy glass to its case, he slowly crawled on his stomach in the direction he heard the horse. There it was, a beautiful Blue Roan. He told himself when this was over he would return and take the horse for himself. Porter remained hidden for another thirty minutes, watching and waiting for the rider to return. When no one showed, he carefully advanced on the horse and put his hand on his rump to keep him calm. Porter noticed the rifle boot was empty. He didn't find a body, so he knew the man wasn't dead. As that thought entered his mind, Porter quickly dropped to the ground. He might have missed something, and that the man might still be close by or within rifle range. Nothing, standing up he made a quick search of the area. He recognized the saddle as belonging to the hunter, and he knew Bellows or his men did not own this horse. Therefore, the only explanation was that Bellows had failed to kill the hunter. Porter got excited, thinking, *"Finally, a worthy opponent."*

Both men were now on alert for the other. Logan wanted to lead Porter away from the mine and any help his friends might be able to give him. After running for over a half mile he slowed to let his heart beat slow. If he had to take a shot, his body would have to be calm so he could hold a steady bead on his target.

Porter followed the boot tracks away from the horse, but lost them where Logan had switched over to his moccasins. He found the boots laying in the grass behind a fallen log. Porter began searching in a circular pattern to pick up Logan's tracks. It was getting dark when he found the slightest imprint on a rotted log suggesting his target was headed east.

As the sun set, all the gun fire back at the mine had ceased. Logan and Porter have stopped for the night. Sound carried much farther in the night and neither man wanted to give away his position.

Charlie and Gideon switched places guarding the mine during the night. Even though they had both got some sleep, the tension and their age has taken its toll, not to mention they were low on ammunition and food. "Charlie, where do you think Logan went?"

"I don't know, but he's out there doing what has to be done. We just have to hold out until he comes for us."

Spivey didn't understand why they were wasting time with these two old coots. "Boss, why don't we just ride to California? We got better than a hundred and fifty thousand dollars from that bank the other night. With our other takes, we got more than the two hundred thousand you wanted."

"Because that old miner I shot back in the gorge can identify us. We only go to jail if we're caught for robbery, but we'll hang for murder if he lives. We can't leave any witnesses behind."

The shooting at the mine was sporadic. Charlie and Gideon would fire a single shot every so often. More to let Hickey know they were still alive and alert, than to hit anything.

Marsh was getting anxious. "Why don't we just rush them Boss?"

"Because they are to well protected behind that wall and would pick us off. When Porter gets back he can get to higher ground and pick them off."

Logan and Porter were now too far away from the mine to hear any shooting that might be going on back at the mine. Both men were on the move at sunup. Logan decided to start climbing higher. Porter was uncomfortable having to be the chaser. He was concerned that he could come under his adversary's sights at any time. It was that thought that made him change his tactics. He quit trying to trail McCart and headed due north to circle around and get above him.

Neither man knew it, but they were now headed on a path that would bring them together. It was now well into the afternoon and Logan sat down to rest. He knew he had to stop running and being hunted, and start thinking about being the hunter. He had just finished a piece of jerky, and was washing it down with a drink from his canteen when he heard the sound. It was the sound of metal striking stone. A sound he had heard on more than one occasion. Porter had made the first mistake, one that would save Logan's life. While he was getting into position his rifle slipped from his sweaty hands, and it struck the rock he was going to use as a rest for his rifle.

Logan kept the canteen up to his lips. Because Logan hadn't moved, Porter believed his prey hadn't heard the sound of his rifle striking the rock. Just as he was squeezing the trigger Logan rolled over backwards, and dropped behind the log he was sitting on. The bullet whizzed over his head.

Porter swore softly, "Damn, I missed him again. This cat has nine lives for sure." While Porter was chambering another round into the breech, Logan was on the move. He quickly covered a hundred feet on his hands and knees. Wanting distance between him and his pursuer he hadn't bothered to be quiet. He knew Porter would be reloading for another shot, so he flattened out and rolled to his right. The bullet thudded into the ground where he had been a second earlier. Logan stood and ran as fast as his legs would carry him, weaving between the trees. He dipped down into a ravine and started north at a dead run. The ravine headed up the mountain and Logan was hopeful it would allow him to get in front his attacker. He was laboring from running up hill in the thin air. He stopped to catch his breath and calm his leg muscles that were screaming from the pain of running up hill.

Porter was angry with himself for having missed McCart with both shots. He would have to be more careful with McCart now on high alert. Although he believes he still has the advantage with his Sharps. Porter thinks McCart is armed with a Henry repeater, even so, it would only take one well placed shot to kill him if he got to close. Porter moved down to where he had last seen McCart to pick up his tracks.

Logan was regaining his strength and was searching the terrain as he rested. It was behind a stand of huckleberry that he saw a dark depression. The sun was screened out by the forest canopy, ruling out the possibility that it was shade from the bushes. He started climbing for the stand of huckleberry, being careful to not leave any sign of his movements. Slipping in behind the bushes he found a small cave. It was large enough to stand up in, but only went back about ten feet. The distance up the hill to the cave was misleading from below. Looking back down into the ravine he estimated he was about five hundred yards above the rock he had sat on to rest.

Porter was searching the ravine where Logan had disappeared. He found a couple of foot prints where the leaves had been disturbed leading back up the mountain. It would be dark soon, so he decided to stop there for the night.

It was now dark and Logan hadn't seen any sign of Porter. He grabbed the LeMat out of his saddle holster, and leaving everything else in the cave he stepped outside. If he ran across something in the dark, the shotgun barrel on the LeMat would eliminate the need to take careful aim before shooting, or clearly identifying his attacker. Scouting around in the dark was difficult, but something Logan had done many times as a kid, and in the army during the civil war. There was a deer path that ran past the cave from the floor of the ravine to the top of the ridge. While it provided an escape route, it was too thin to offer any protection, or provide cover against a skilled marksman like Porter. After traveling a short distant up, he retraced his steps and passed the cave to go back down into the ravine. He returned to the rock where he had stopped to rest and first saw the cave.

The air was crisp, and dew would fall over the evening hours. The wet leaves would disguise the footfalls of any tracks he might accidently leave. Logan wanted to set up some kind of warning system to let him know of Porter's arrival. But Porter had proven to be a good tracker, and would most likely see any obstacles placed in his path to warn against his approach. The trick would be to determine the path his stalker would travel. Then develop a method to sound the alarm. As he was sitting on the same rock as he had earlier in the day, it became clear that the rock he was sitting on was the best place to set up the trap. If his pursuer was tracking him, he would come straight up the ravine as he had done and to this same spot.

As a child Logan had trapped many rabbits in his snares. He decided to use the same concept for his warning system. After searching around with his hands, he found a vine and cut off a length of about six feet. Then he cut some very thin green leaf limbs to use as rope. He broke a branch off the dead fall laying beside the rock. Using the branch, which had a V at the end of it, he stuck it into the hill just past the rock. Not to deep, only enough so it would stand on its own with a little pressure on top of it. Carefully he brushed the leaves away, then he suspended the vine about an inch off the ground, and covered it with leaves as if the ground had never been disturbed. He intertwined the thin green limbs, tied one end to the vine and the other to the bottom of a stick. He placed the stick so it laid at a sixty degree angle through the V of the limb he had stuck into the hill. Then he cut a hole into the bottom of a deadfall. Carefully aligning the stick and the hole in the deadfall, he lowered the deadfall onto the stick. Lastly he covered the trip limbs with leaves to hide them from view. If it worked, anyone approaching the rock would step on the vine pulling out the stick, and causing the dead fall to crash down and hit the ground with a thud. As he returned to the cave he collected some small stones, and carried them back with him.

Porter was sure McCart had not backtracked during the evening. Still, using his spy glass he scanned the hills behind him for any sign of McCart. Once again he was placed in the uncomfortable position of having to track his prey instead of laying in wait. Slowly, he started up the ravine, using the trees and rocks for cover as he trailed his prey. Stopping every so often to scan the hills with his spy glass.

Logan opened his eyes. He had slept deeper and later than normal as a result of the previous days strenuous running. Laying very still he quietly listened to the sounds outside the cave. Not hearing anything unusual he crawled to the front and looked out over the ravine. His pursuer was no where in sight. Protected by the cave and darkness, any attack had been highly unlikely during the night. Now all he has to do is wait patiently until Porter arrived.

Logan was sitting back in the cave chewing on a piece of jerky, more for the salt to satisfy his strained leg muscles than to satisfy any hunger. As he was thinking of day's past, he heard the deadfall hit the ground. Quickly he crawled to the front of the cave and looked down into the ravine. No one was in sight. It could have been an animal that tripped the snare, but Logan doubted that. He was glad he had emptied his rifle of its old load that morning and reloaded it with fresh powder and ball. In addition, he had found a limb approximately six feet long, perfect for steadying his rifle while taking aim.

Porter realized exactly what he'd done as he stepped on the covered vine and heard the deadfall hit the ground. He immediately plastered himself against the side of the hill behind a rock. Now that the leaves had been disturbed by its action, he could see the snare laying on the ground, and how it had been rigged. Porter admired the ingenuity shown by McCart, and once again understood the intelligence and ability of his prey. The trap was only meant to be a warning. It posed no actual threat, and was not capable of catching any animals. That meant McCart was still in the area, and Porter had no doubts that one of them would die here this morning.

Logan was confident that he was well concealed, and that Porter was within range of his Hawken Musket. At over five hundred yards, he would have to make his first shot count, or risk being trapped inside the cave. He had never fired his Hawken around Hickey and his men, and couldn't be sure whether Porter knew he was carrying it or not. The odds are that Porter only thinks he has his Henry repeater. His one advantage was that he could stand up in the cave to take a shot, while remaining hidden from view.

Porter slipped back behind some larger rocks where he could move around while staying under cover. He was keeping close watch on the hillsides through his spyglass. He was searching for movement, or anything that stood out from the natural terrain. He has laid in wait many times to kill his victims. It was not in him to be impatient, a trait he was hoping McCart didn't have.

It's been approximately two hours since the snare was tripped. Logan knew Porter was down there somewhere, but he hadn't seen any sign of him. Under normal conditions Logan could outwait a flower trying to bloom in winter, but time was becoming critical, he had to end this and get back to help Charlie and Gideon. It had been more than two days now that this cat and mouse game had been going on. He wasn't sure how much longer they could hold out at the mine. Picking up one of the stones he had carried back to the cave, he softly tossed it out and down the hill about fifty feet in front of him. He was hoping Porter would raise up to look towards the sound.

It worked, Porter looked up over the rocks he was hidden behind to see what had stirred the bushes. Then he quickly slid back down behind the rocks and out of sight, thinking to himself. *"I can't believe I fell for that old trick."*

Logan still had to get Porter to raise up high enough to take aim from behind the rocks. It was likely that even then he would only raise his head enough to take a shot. It would be a small target, but he had no other choice. He took the LeMat out of his gun belt and switched it over to the pistol cylinder. The LeMat was a.44 caliber just like his Remington revolver and Henry repeater. But it had a much louder report than his revolver and sounded much more like his rifle. If he could make Porter believe he only had his Henry rifle, which would be well out of range, he might be able to get Porter to try a shot. Logan fired the LeMat pistol with the bullet falling far short of Porter's location.

Logan quickly grabbed his Hawken and placed it on top of the limb for support, then he sighted down the hill and waited for Porter to show his head. Porter was grinning while thinking of the advantage his Sharps gave him over his opponents Henry rifle. Feeling safe, Porter laid his Sharps across the rocks and aimed up the hill into huckleberry bushes covering the mouth of the cave. Logan aimed about an inch high to compensate for the distance. Porter never had another thought as the bullet struck him dead center in the middle of his forehead.

Logan eased down the hill. All the while keeping an eye on Porters position in case he was playing possum. When he got within thirty feet, he could see Porters brains splattered all over the leaves. Picking up the Sharps, and grabbing the ammunition belt off Porters body, he headed back toward the mine. Not having to worry about Porter anymore he was able to get back in one day. He found Blue cropping in the stand of trees where he had left him.

Chapter 27

Logan was awake before the sun rose. He needed to find out if Charlie and Gideon were still alive. There had been no activity overnight, and he didn't know if Hickey and his men were still held up in the rocks.

Logan left his rifles at camp and moved up over the top of the mine. He slowly slid down on his belly to look over the top of the mine entrance. He was surprised to see no one guarding the entrance. Not knowing where anyone was he couldn't call out. Grabbing a couple of small stones he started dropping them onto the wall protecting the entrance. After tossing down a couple stones he stopped and waited for a reaction. No one responded or came out to see what was happening.

Logan was concerned both men might have been killed. Just as he started to work his way back up the hill, he heard a low muttering. Taking a chance he softly spoke down to the mine. "Charlie, is that you?"

The response was low and labored, "Logan?"

"Charlie, what's wrong, are you both okay?"

"Gideon caught a bullet in his shoulder and is bleeding pretty bad, and we are out of food, water, and ammunition."

"Where is Hickey and his men?"

"Last I knew they were still holed up down in those rocks. They usually start shooting just after sunup. I think they know we are out of ammunition."

"Wait close to the entrance, I'll be right back with some supplies."

Logan worked his way back to his camp and put together a small pack that included jerky, water, and ammunition. Then he searched around and found some moss. After grabbing the rope off his saddle, he picked up the small pack of supplies he'd put together along with the Sharps, and headed back atop the mine. With the supplies and rifle he was carrying, it took all his strength not to slide off the steep slope. Using the rope he lowered the supply pack and rifle down to the entrance. "Charlie, there is some moss in the pack. Wet it down and place it over Gideon's wound. Give me about five minutes to get back and fire a couple shots down into the rocks at Hickey."

"Why shoot?"

"So he will know your not out of ammunition to keep him from rushing you. Also, with any luck he will fire back giving me a bead on his location.

Logan was just returning to his camp when he heard Charlie fire a couple shots. He waited to hear Hickey's return fire. No luck, there was no return fire. This worried Logan, because it meant Hickey was probably moving up on the mine.

Hickey and Spivey were moving up to the mine from the side along the river bank. "Boss, those shots came from the mine. That means they aren't out of ammunition like we thought."

Hickey looked over at Spivey and showed his irritation. "That doesn't mean anything. They probably saved a couple rounds just to make us think they are well armed. But we will wait awhile and see if they fire again."

Charlie moved back into the mine and started changing the dressing on Gideon's wound. After wiping away the blood, he moistened the moss and placed it over the wound. Gideon was weak and remained asleep while Charlie tended to his wound. After tending to Gideon, Charlie sat back and drank deep from the canteen Logan had provided him. Then he tore into a couple pieces of jerky.

Retrieving his Henry rifle, Logan began circling behind the rocks Hickey and his men had been using for cover. He saw their horses, but the rocks appeared empty. Then Marsh moved, alerting Logan to his presence. Since he had re-supplied Charlie with ammunition, Logan could take his time taking Hickey and his men. Moving up between the horses he could see Marsh was alone. Checking the packs on the horses, he found the cash and gold stolen from the assay office and mines. Quietly laying his rifle on the ground. There was too much distance to cover before Marsh would realize his presence, and firing a shot would put Hickey on notice of his return. Logan drew and threw his knife in one fluid motion, hitting Marsh in the back of his neck. Logan quickly ran to Marsh to finish him. But his concerns of Marsh yelling out were erased when he got to him. Logan's knife had gone all the way through Marsh's neck, severing his spine and killing him instantly.

He released the ropes holding the packs and let them drop to the ground. Logan froze when the packs dropped and made a loud thud as they hit the ground. After making sure no one was around to hear the sound of the packs falling, he dragged them back into the trees. Covering the packs with rocks and leaves, using some small stones he marked the spot with his circle M brand. He returned to the horses and wiped out the drag marks made by the heavy packs and his feet.

Logan returned his focus to Hickey and Spivey. He entered the rocks and found the coffee pot still on the hot stones next to the fire. Picking up an empty mug he poured himself a cup of coffee, then searched the tracks around camp. The freshest tracks led down to the river. That meant Hickey and Spivey were working their way up the mine along the river. Probably wanting to use its rushing waters to mask any sound of their approach.

Spivey was getting jittery. "Boss, there hasn't been any more firing from the mine. What do you want to do?"

Hickey was wishing Porter was back, he could pepper the mine with his Sharps rifle and root them out. "I don't know Spivey. Now quit your whining and let me think." The mine was well protected by that wall. Hickey knew if they did have any ammunition left, the odds of being shot while charging them were pretty high. "Spivey, I want you to sneak up to that wall and see if you can tell what they're doing."

"Boss, that will put me in the open. I could be shot."

"I'll shoot you if you don't get moving."

Spivey left the river bank and slowly made his way through the trees toward the mine. He knew Hickey was using him as bait, and he wasn't about to get shot if he could help it. As he worked his way through the forest, he considered heading back to camp and riding out. Spivey was close to the tree line at the mine when he stopped to look at the small circle of stones with an "M" in the middle. He thought it was some kind of claim marker identifying the boundaries of the mine. Not understanding its purpose he took another step. When his foot fell into the hole, the stakes drove up through his foot and calf. He started screaming in pain, "Hickey, I'm hurt. Help me."

Hickey was confused, because there hadn't been any shots. His mind was racing and he started to think to himself. *They must have captured Spivey, and are forcing him to yell out to draw me in closer.* He had no idea that Spivey had stepped into a trap. Hickey continued to think the situation through. *"Porter must be dead, otherwise he would have returned by now. There is more than two hundred thousand dollars back at camp, and it's all mine. What do I care if some old geezer can testify that I shot him. Hell, he probably won't live much longer anyway. I need to gather the horses and get out now."* Hickey left the river, taking a more direct route back to the horses and money.

Logan heard the scream as he was working his way up the river, and thought. *"Hickey or Spivey must have stepped into one of my perimeter traps."* There hadn't been any gunfire, so I knew the man hadn't been shot. The trap would not kill him, unless he bled out or died from infection. But either of those instances would take time, and the man was still screaming for help. Working my way up the river I found the tracks where Hickey and Spivey had waited along the river. The tracks of only one man lead toward the mine. The other set of tracks, which he recognized as Hickey's, were headed back to their horses. Logan chuckled as he thought about Hickey's response when he found his money missing.

Hickey was furious. He was searching behind every tree and rock looking for the packs filled with money. All that was left was a thousand dollars he had placed in his saddlebags. Marsh was laying dead in the rocks. He found himself talking out loud. "McCart, you are a dead man. I am going to kill you if it is the last thing I do."

I was making my way through the trees when I saw Spivey. He was bent over in an awkward position with his leg stuck in the hole, and the spikes had driven themselves all the way through his foot. "Mister, you are hurt pretty bad. If you don't let me help you, you are going to die."

Spivey didn't recognize the voice. He knew it wasn't Hickey or Marsh. "Who are you?"

"I am Sheriff McCart out of Tin Cup. Do I come in and help, or do I move on and let you die stuck in that hole?"

"Some choice, die here or hang back in Tin Cup."

"Maybe you will get lucky, and they will just send you to prison."

"Alright Sheriff, come on in. I don't fancy gettin' eaten by wolves or a bear while I'm stuck in this damn hole."

Logan moved in closer while keeping behind the trees for cover. "Throw your gun over here." Spivey tossed his revolver into the trees toward Logan's voice. "Now the rifle."

Spivey tossed his rifle away as he spoke. "That's it Sheriff, I promise. Now please, come and get me out of this hole."

Logan walked up covering Spivey with his pistol. "Got any knives or any other weapons on you?"

"No, I give up. Just get my leg off these spikes and stop the bleeding."

Logan holstered his revolver and bent down to get a closer look at Spivey's foot.

"Admiring your handiwork, Sheriff?"

"No, I am trying to figure the best way to get your foot free without causing anymore damage. Take your shirt off, and hand it to me."

"It's a little cold to be going without a shirt up here don't you think."

"When I pull your foot off those spikes I am going to have to plug the holes. So unless you are carrying a passel of bandages with you, give me the shirt." Spivey removed his shirt and handed it to Logan. Picking up a downed tree limb, Logan hoisted Spivey up to a standing position. "Here, use this limb as a crutch, and bite down on this stick. I am going to pull your leg straight up to draw the spikes out." Just as Spivey started to ask a question, Logan pulled hard and fast, removing the foot from the spikes. Spivey didn't get a chance to ask his question. He passed out from the pain. Logan plugged the holes with strips from Spivey's shirt.

Even if Spivey was to wake up he wouldn't be going anywhere in his condition. Logan retrieved Spivey's guns and moved to the tree line and yelled out. "Charlie, it's Logan, I'm coming in."

Charlie moved to the entrance to greet him. "Man, we've sure missed you. What's going on out there? I heard a blood curdling scream."

"Spivey was nice enough to put one of my traps to the test. He didn't like the results. Here, take these weapons, I have to go get him."

"You're not bringing him in here are you?"

"It's alright, he isn't a danger anymore."

Logan hefted Spivey over his shoulder and carried him to the mine. After laying him down he walked over to take a look at Gideon. "Charlie, go down and fetch a pail of water."

"What about Hickey, ain't he still out there?"

"If he is, he's looking for his money. You'll be safe, now hurry." The fire was down to coals, so Logan added a large log and got the fire blazing hot.

Charlie returned with the water. "I picked up some more moss off the trees down by the river in case you needed some more."

"Thanks Charlie, we are going to need it." Logan stuck his knife into the fire, and while it heated up, he cleaned Gideon's wound.

Gideon opened his eyes to see Logan fussing over him. "Seems like every time you show up, I have been shot."

"Quiet, you need to save your strength. I have to cut that bullet out of your shoulder or you will die of lead poisoning. Sorry I don't have any whiskey for you."

"Do what needs doing, I trust you."

Logan handed Charlie Spivey's shirt, "Charlie, wet some of that moss down, and cut some squares and strips off that shirt to hold the moss to Gideon's shoulder. While Charlie cut up the shirt, Logan cut open a couple cartridges in preparation for using the powder. "Charlie, stand over me with that canteen and rinse the blood away as I dig out the bullet." Gideon passed out as Logan dug into his shoulder. After removing the bullet, Logan poured gunpowder into the wound. Then touched it off with a burning stick from the fire. "Charlie, grab the moss and strips you cut from the shirt." The flash of gunpowder stopped the bleeding and Logan dressed the wound with the moss. We will wait here for a couple of days and let him regain his strength. Then I'll get him to the doctor in Tin Cup.

During the next two days Logan helped Charlie clean up. Logan shot a deer so they had plenty of meat. After smoking the meat they hung it back in the cave where it was cool. Spivey died on the third day from infection of his wounds.

Logan was preparing to take Gideon to the doctor in Tin Cup when Charlie asked. "What about Hickey, he got away with all the money and might still be hunting you?"

"I had forgotten all about the money. Charlie, cinch up the sawbuck saddle on Thor and follow me." When they got down to the rocks Logan went straight to where he had buried the money packs. It was still there. "Let's load these up."

Charlie could only look on in amazement. "How in tarnation did you get these packs away from Hickey?"

"I killed Marsh and unloaded it while Hickey and Spivey were sneaking up on you along the river. I'm willing to bet Hickey is still around and that he wants me dead." Logan removed twenty thousand dollars and gave it to Gideon. That's the amount Hickey had taken from him back at the Royal Gorge.

Since Thor was weighted down with the money packs, Logan hoisted Gideon up on Blue. Mounting up on one of the horses taken from Hickey's men, he took Gideon to Tin Cup. Charlie remained at the mine to protect it until Logan and Gideon returned.

The doctor was giving Gideon an examination of his wound. "I don't know who patched you up Gideon, but he did a fine job. I will just sew the hole up and give you something for the pain."

"That's okay Doc, I'm feelin' pretty good. The pain ain't nothin' a good stiff drink of whiskey won't fix."

While Gideon was at the doctor's office, Logan returned the stolen money to the assay office. He requested that they act as the proper agent and distribute the money to the mines. He instructed them to try and locate the relatives of Two Time Benny, and send them the extra fifteen thousand that Hickey's men had mined.

All of the town's folk and business owners were pleased that Logan had recovered the stolen money. Everyone was trying to buy him drinks, and the town council voted to give him a reward. Logan accepted a few drinks, but he refused to accept any reward. Logan and Gideon remained in town for a couple days to let Gideon rest up and heal to the Doctor's satisfaction before heading back to the mine with fresh supplies.

Randy was still being cared for by the doctor. He was out of danger and was going to live. Although he was still to weak to travel. Logan convinced him it was best to remain behind under the doctor's care.

Chapter 28

Charlie was happy to see Logan and Gideon ride up to the mine. "Logan, I ain't sure, but I think someone has been stalking around out beyond the trees. I have stayed holed up inside the mine since you left."

"You did the right thing, it's probably Hickey. I am sure he is still in the area. Let's get these supplies unloaded and I'll have a look around." The tracks were two days old, but they were Hickey's alright. The star in the hoof print was clearly visible.

They were enjoying the stew Gideon made when Logan inquired about how much gold they had mined. "How is the mining going, are you still pulling anything out of the main vein?"

Charlie was the one who responded. "No, the vein we found is all played out. Gideon thinks there is another one in there somewhere, but he and I have talked about calling it quits."

Logan was surprised to hear that, "Any idea about how much you have taken out?"

"We figure it to be close to a million dollars." Logan gasped out loud. "Are you kidding me? You boys are rich, what are you going to do with all that money?"

Gideon reminded Logan, "You mean we are rich. Remember Logan, you are an equal partner. What do you think we should do, stay or pull up stakes?"

Logan thought about that last question for a minute before answering. "I think we should start pack the gold to the assay office and turn it into cash. That much gold is too heavy to carry out. And if we are going to call it quits, then we should sell the mine. We should get a reasonable price for it after they see the quantity and quality of the gold you mined. First things first, I will go into Tin Cup and file a proper claim under Gideon's name. Everyone knows he has a mine out here, and since they have seen him in town now, ownership will not be in dispute. I'll bring back some extra leather packs for transporting the gold. In the mean time, you two stay holed up here in the mine under cover. Hickey will be hunting me, and he wouldn't hesitate to use you two to get to me. He has to know the mine has produced a good bit of gold. But my instincts tell me he won't attack until after we turn it into cash.

Before leaving, Logan killed an Elk and brought extra water up into the mine. Charlie and Gideon cut and stacked extra firewood. "You two can smoke and salt that meat while I am gone. But make sure one of you is always standing guard.

Logan could feel he was being watched as he returned to Tin Cup, causing him to think to himself. *"I'm sure Hickey won't make his move until we have cashed in the gold. He wants me dead something fierce, but he also needs the cash."*

After arriving in Tin Cup Logan headed straight for the land registrar's office. He filed the mine under Gideon's name. Walking out of the office he posted the mine for sale on the bulletin board located out on the porch. Before heading to the saloon for a much needed beer, he went to the assay office and cashed in a small pouch of gold he had brought back with him. He wanted any prospective buyers to know the quality of gold they had mined.

Dan Clady was sitting at a table nursing a beer when Logan walked in. "Mind if I sit?"

Dan looked up with a smile on his face. "Please do. You saved a lot of people around here from ruin by recovering that money. The town has decided to increase your salary by offering you free supplies and staples for as long as your sheriff."

"Well, that is very kind of them, but I have come to resign my position as sheriff."

"Why, you can have anything you want?"

"My partners and I have decided to cash in and head back down off the mountain. I posted the mine for sale. If you know anyone interested, I would be obliged if you would send them over to see me."

"A lot of people are going to be sorry to see you leave, Logan."

Logan handed Clady his badge and left. He headed up the street to collect his belongings and Sallie, which were still at the cabin. He stopped off at the general store on his way out of town to purchase some extra leather bags for transporting the gold.

His last stop was at the doctor's office. He could hear Randy complaining before he got through the front door. As he entered, Randy started giving him what for, "Logan, I can't just lay around here like some dead log in the forest. Take me to the mine with you."

Logan looked over at the Doc, who was shaking his head no. "Randy, I will be back in a couple days. If Doc say's you're ready, you can come then."

"Alright, but I don't like it none." That wasn't altogether truthful. Randy was still feeling the effects of being shot, and he was a little relieved Logan had refused to take him along.

Hickey was maintaining a fair distance behind. He kept an eye on Logan using the spy glass he took off Porter's body, that he had found in the ravine where Logan killed him. He wanted McCart dead, but he was going to wait until they converted the gold into cash. Hickey had slipped into town and read the sale notice Logan posted outside the registrar's office. That meant it would not be long before they pulled up stakes.

The ride back to the mine had been uneventful, but Logan still couldn't shake the feeling he was being followed. After unloading the packs he went up into the mine and presented his plan to his partners. "There is too much gold to transport in a single trip. I think I should pack half of it to Tin Cup myself, and we can take the other half to town on our way out of the Pass."

Chuckling, Gideon asked, "Do you think we can trust you?" Laughing, they all agreed to the plan.

The next morning they packed up half the gold. It took them a couple of hours to complete the task. When they were done, Logan gave Charlie and Gideon the usual instructions about standing guard and staying alert. He rode away leading four horses and three mules, all loaded down with gold.

Hickey had been watching the whole time. He couldn't believe the amount of gold packed onto the animals. He licked his lips thinking about how rich he was going to be.

As Logan rode into town everyone stepped out into the street to watch the parade of horses and mules stroll down the street. It was no secret he was packing gold. News of his arrival and what he was packing had traveled well ahead of him, and spread quickly. Not wanting to temp anyone, he rode straight to the assay office. Upon entering the office he came face-to-face with Mr. Youngblood. "Good evening Mr. Youngblood."

"Good evening Mr. Hayes, or should I call you McCart now?"

"Logan will do just fine."

"That is some mule train you have out there."

"Yes sir, we did alright for ourselves."

"I saw you posted the mine for sale. Is it still available?"

"Yes sir, are you interested?"

"I don't know, do you think there is any gold left?"

"I think an outfit with the proper equipment and workforce will find it's still very profitable."

"Coming from anyone else, I would take that to be merely a boast, to entice some unsuspecting buyer to purchase a mine that is all played out. But coming from you, I believe it to be true. How about we sit down after you conclude your business here."

"I can meet you over at the saloon if that is okay with you?"

"Very well, I will meet you there."

The assay office employed several more guards after the robbery. With their help Logan carried the packs of gold inside to be converted into cash. When the tally was all done, the total came to just over six hundred thousand dollars. The manager of the assay office was astounded at the purity of the gold. "Mr. McCart, that is a lot of money, do you want us to put it in your packs?"

"No, I would like you to hold it for me. I will be bringing in another load a couple days from now. We can decide how to handle the distribution at that time." The manager of the assay office was astounded to learn there was more. This was by far the richest strike in the Pass. "I am trusting you to remain silent about the amount of this deposit, and that there is more to come."

"You have my word. Mr. McCart. But before you leave, I need to know what you want done with the other six thousand dollars I am holding for you? A man named Stoney, from the Walker mine, came in to collect their share of the stolen money, and after I gave it to him, he handed me back six thousand dollars to hold for you. Said to thank you, and that you would understand."

"Thanks, please hold it with the rest until I return. The money is re-payment for a loan I provided Stoney and his partners."

Logan walked into the saloon, but before sitting down with Mr. Youngblood he spoke across the room. "Pike, bring a beer and a whiskey for Mr. Youngblood and myself."

"Sure thing Sheriff, I mean, Mr. McCart."

Mr. Youngblood thanked Logan for the drinks, but was wanting to get down to business. "That was quite a bit of gold you brought in, what was the total?"

"I'd prefer to keep that a secret if you don't mind?"

"Very well, but how am I supposed to make a proper offer if I can't assess my expected returns?"

Any mining operation is a Gamble Mr. Youngblood. Purchasing the Gideon mine will not be any different."

"I suppose you have a point there, but with the lack of any substantial figures to base my offer on, I am afraid I am only prepared to offer you $2,500. I am sure you can understand my position as a business man."

"What if I was to give you a guarantee against your investment? Would you be willing to up your offer?"

"I suppose so, depending on the terms."

"Mr. Youngblood, I will sell you the mine for one hundred thousand dollars. In return, I will give you my personal guarantee that you will produce over a million dollars in gold from the mine. If you don't, I will refund you the full purchase price. That is a win-win proposition for you."

"That is some guarantee Logan. One I don't think you would make unless you truly believed the mine was still profitable. I will have the documents drawn up. We can sign them at the registrar's office tomorrow morning."

"Great, tomorrow morning then."

Logan left the saloon and went down to Mabel's for dinner. Clady was already seated and motioned him over. "Please, sit and have dinner with me."

Logan took a seat as Mabel was setting a coffee cup in front him. She poured as she asked, "Usual Sheriff, a large steak with potatoes and beans?"

"Yes, thank you Mabel."

Clady inquired as to Logan's plans. "Now that you and your partners are rich, where do you plan on going?"

"First off, I was hoping you would let me use that cabin tonight, Dan. I have business over at the registrar's office in the morning."

"I heard you sold your mine to Mr. Youngblood. That was some guarantee you gave him. Quite a risk on your part don't you think?"

"News travels fast. I don't believe it's a risk at all Dan, none at all."

"What about Hickey, do you think he's still in the area?"

"I do, but you and the town have no more reason to fear him. He is after me, and once our business is concluded he will either be dead, or left the country for good. Now that the mines and the town have implemented stronger security measures, there's no future for him here anymore." They finished their meals in silence and bid each other goodnight.

The next morning I met Mr. Youngblood at the registrar's office and concluded the sale of Gideon's mine.

"Logan, if you ever change your mind, my offer as Vice President of mining operations will remain open."

"Thanks, I'll keep it in mind." Logan stuffed the draft for a hundred thousand dollars in his saddlebags and rode out of town. He didn't stop to talk to Randy, because he would make to much of a fuss about riding back with him. Besides, a couple more day's with Doc wouldn't hurt him.

Hickey watched as Logan placed something in his saddlebags and rode out. There was no reason to wait any longer. He would ambush him on the way back to the mine, and steal the money. As he mounted up he said to himself, *"After I kill McCart, and those two old coots, I'll ride to California a free, rich man."* Hickey had no idea Logan wasn't carrying any real cash. Not ever having had any real business with a bank, he wasn't all that familiar with bank drafts.

There was no doubt in Logan's mind that Hickey was out there watching, so he left the trail and started riding trough the forest. The going was much slower, but he was re-assured by the fact that the trees helped provide him cover. Stopping to rest, he dismounted and took the time to watch his back trail while taking a drink from his canteen. Logan decided if he had to move quickly, he didn't want the mules and horses slowing him down. So he re-arranged the horse and mules. He tied Blue's lead rope to Sallies pack saddle, then the others in kind. Sallie would follow Dusty's trail and return to the mine with the others in tow.

Hickey was watching as Logan fussed with his animals. It didn't make any sense, why would he release the pack animals if they were carrying all that money. It hit him like a barn had fallen on him, Logan left the money in the care of the assay office. That meant there was still more gold at the mine, and they had to make another trip to Tin Cup. Probably their last as they left the Pass. Hickey couldn't afford any more mistakes. He decided to kill Logan now, take his pack animals, and pack the remaining gold to California. He followed until the lead mule had dropped back and was out of McCart's view. Riding in from behind he moved up along Sallie and took hold of her lead rope that was looped around the pack saddle. Dismounting he tied Sallie to a large pine tree. Making a quick search of the packs, it was as he thought, no money, only a few supplies. Mounting up he headed after McCart. He could return and pick up the pack animals later.

Logan could no longer hear the footfalls of the pack train. But he paid it no mind knowing Sallie would keep coming. He pulled up to get his bearings, and without notice Dusty reared up, causing Logan's head to hit a low limb, which knocked him out. Dusty charged off from the bullet hitting him in the rear flank. Hickey had misjudged his shot. He failed to adjust for shooting down hill from such a long distance. He was confident he had hit McCart. He didn't realize he had only hit his horse, and that was what caused him to rear up and dump his rider. Thinking McCart was dead, Hickey headed to the mine.

Chapter 29

Slowly regaining consciousness, Logan opened his eyes. The pain in his head was throbbing something fierce. It was dark and he was cold and wet from the evening dew. Laying still he gathered his thoughts trying to figure out where he was and what had happened. His head was full of cobwebs, but as it started to clear he remembered Dusty rearing up, the report of the bullet, and his head slamming into that large limb he was now staring at right above him. Feeling his head he felt a big knot on top. It was throbbing and he winced as he touched the spot covered with dried blood. Sitting up he reached over and grabbed his hat laying off to the side. He was trying to regain his legs under him, while thinking about Hickey ambushing him.

I am really getting tired of being clubbed in the head. I'm not dead, so Hickey must not have checked to confirm his kill again. That meant he would be headed back to the mine to kill Charlie and Gideon. As much as I wanted to start a fire to get warm and dry out. I couldn't waste time. Charlie and Gideon are going to need my help.

It would take me better than a day to walk back to the mine, even in good light. I decided to backtrack and find Sallie. I had been walking for about a hour when I found her and the others tied up. It was still dark, and aside from Blue being spooked, the terrain was to rough to trust him. So I removed the packsaddle from Sallie, and tied Blue to the tree with the other horses and mules still tethered to him. Heaving myself up on to

Sallie I headed to the mine. Sallie was sure footed, and even in the dark we were making good time.

Hickey had made it back to the mine before dark. Not wanting to waste any time he yelled out to the mine. "You two up there, McCart is dead. If you want to live you will throw your guns out and walk down here with your hands raised."

Charlie and Gideon looked at each other with worried faces. "You don't believe him do you Charlie?"

"I don't know. It doesn't seem possible. But why would he come back here if he didn't believe Logan was dead?"

"I don't know either. In any case, I don't think he will let us live to tell anyone what happened."

"I agree Gideon. We have to stall and hope help comes." Charlie moved to the front of the mine, and yelled out. "We don't believe you. What assurance do we have that you will let us live?"

"All I want is the gold you still have stashed up there with you. If you come out and give me the gold, I'll let you live. Then you can go collect your money McCart left with the assay office. You have until morning to decide. After that I'll come in shooting." Believing there was no more threat from McCart, Hickey started a fire and rolled out his bed roll.

"Charlie, what do we do?"

"We get some sleep and deal with it in the morning. I'll take the first watch."

Sallie steadily moved forward, making her way through the dark and over the rough terrain. Albeit, somewhat slower than I wanted, the fact was, she was making better time than I could have made on foot. Her sure footedness, and ability to see in the dark was far superior to mine. At this pace we should make it back to the mine before sunup.

Before reaching the mine I turned Sallie to the west, and headed for the Taylor River. I doubted Hickey would take the long way around, and I didn't much like the idea of riding into another ambush. Reaching the river I kept Sallie in the soft sand of the river bank. Moving up into the trees I jumped down from Sallie's back. It was still dark and there was nothing I could do for the time being, except find a good position from which to watch. One that would give me a clear view of the mine entrance and the open ground in front. Moving to the tree line I saw the campfire on the other side of the compound just inside the trees.

The fire had to be Hickey's. He believed I was dead, and knowing Charlie and Gideon would not be a threat, he wasn't concerned about having a fire. At that moment I kind of envied him. I wanted a fire in the worst way to get warm and finish drying out. Not to mention missing my hot coffee. Stepping back into the trees I moved down into the rocks where Hickey had set up the last time. From this position I had a good field of fire and could cover the mine and open yard.

Gideon had fallen asleep on watch, and was awakened by Hickey yelling at them. "What about it fellas, do you come out peaceful like, or do I come up and get you?"

Gideon responded by firing a shot at the voice. Hickey swore as the shot creased his cheek. In response he fired four quick shots off the side walls of the mine. He was hoping the shots would ricochet and hit the man who had fired at him. Gideon scrambled on his hands and knees back into the mine, while Charlie returned fire to cover his retreat.

They remained inside the mine. It was too dangerous out at the wall with Hickey throwing lead off the side of the mountain to ricochet his shots. Hickey weighed his options, it was to dangerous to attack from the front, and although they might be old men, they could still shoot straight. He noticed they moved back inside the mine abandoning the outside wall. They had restocked their supplies, so he couldn't wait them out. As he was figuring a way to root them out, his anger was growing at the thought it couldn't be done. Suddenly he remembered McCart had delivered guns and supplies to them without entering the mine. Scanning the area above, he noticed a man could crawl down over the top of the mine's entrance. But what good was that, he couldn't drop down into the face of the mine. He would be riddled by bullets before he could gather himself and shoot back. And the distance overlooking the mouth was to great to allow him to lean over and shoot back inside the shaft. His frustration began to mount and he kicked a stone into his campfire. Sparks and a cloud of smoke flew up when the rock crashed into the fire. This gave him the idea that he could smoke them out.

Hickey gathered small twigs and sticks measuring about three feet in length. When he had enough, he bundled them together, then stuffed dry grass and leaves inside the bundle to make it easier to ignite. Picking up his rifle and bundle of sticks, he headed for the top of the mine entrance. As he inched his way down the steep cliff, he gathered some larger limbs, and pushed them along in front him as he inched closer. Reaching the edge, he got himself firmly set so as not to fall over, then he lit a Lucifer and ignited his bundle. As the blaze took hold he dropped it down in front of the mine entrance. Most of the sticks were from pine trees and smoked heavily from the sap. The draft carried the smoke back into the mine. As the fire grew, Hickey continued to feed the fire as he pushed the larger limbs and more leaves down onto the fire.

Smoke filled the mine and Charlie and Gideon began choking and coughing. They couldn't stay in there much longer. Chocking, Charlie yelled out. "We give up, we're coming out."

"Toss your weapons out first."

After tossing their rifles out, Gideon and Charlie started walking out. Hickey was taking aim, and just as he was ready to plug Charlie in the back, a bullet struck his rifle. It hit the receiver and jammed the trigger. It also cut a groove through his thumb, causing him to drop the rifle into the mine. As Hickey was drawing his pistol, Logan began peppering him with lead from his own pistol. None of the shots were hitting Hickey, but he couldn't raise up to get a shot at Charlie or Gideon as they ran for cover.

Once Charlie and Hickey reached the trees, Logan stopped firing. Hickey was in a position that Logan couldn't hit him as long as he held low to the ground. Logan yelled out to Charlie and Gideon, telling them to work their way back to him through the trees, and to stay under cover. The two men were surprised to hear Logan's voice, thinking he was dead. They were making their way through the trees when Charlie grabbed Gideon's arm, and in a sharp voice snapped out, "Stop!"

"What is it?"

"See that marker?" He pointed to the small circle of stones surrounding an "M". "That's Logan's sign indicating a trap."

"You're right, I'd forgotten all about them. We can't stay here, what do we do?"

"Reach down and grab a stick. Poke the ground in front of you as you walk. If the ground cover breaks, stop and go around." Charlie found the trap and left it undisturbed. Continuing on, they probed the ground looking for traps until they arrived at the rocks where Logan was waiting. Charlie grabbed Logan's hand and shook it vigorously, not wanting to let go. "Man, we thought you were dead. Hickey said he killed you."

"He tried, but he hit Dusty instead of me. When Dusty reared up I was knocked out by a tree limb. Hickey thought the shot hit me and didn't bother to verify his kill. A mistake he continues to make."

"What now, do we go after him?"

"Not we, me. I want you two to stay put. I will go up to the mine and retrieve your rifles. Now that he knows he can smoke you out, you'll be better off protecting yourselves inside these rocks." Logan returned with their rifles and couple of canteens full of water. after a few last instructions he set out after Hickey.

Hickey crawled back up the mountain. His anger had returned, and it was directed straight at McCart. He knew McCart would not give up until he had hunted him down and killed him, or he killed McCart. Running was out of the question. If he doesn't kill McCart on this mountain, he will always be watching his back, waiting for the day McCart shows up to kill him.

Logan's own rifle was still in its boot on Dusty's saddle. So he reloaded his pistol, and touched the knife on his gun belt to make sure it was still in its sheath. Logan no longer worried about being ambushed from a distance, because he found Hickey's damaged rifle where it had fallen down into the mine. Whatever happened now would happen within fifty yards of one another. He found himself wishing he was wearing his moccasins. He couldn't worry about that now, he would just have to be more cautious about where he stepped.

The time was tense for both men as they moved in search of one another. Hickey stopped on several occasions to holster his pistol and relieve the pain in his thumb. It was pure luck that it had not been torn off when that bullet hit his rifle. Hickey had always done his fighting from a horse, he knew McCart had the advantage in the forest, and he was being careful not to make a mistake. He knew he had to be as silent as possible if he wanted to live. He had seen first hand how good McCart was in the woods.

Hickey would be like a wounded wolf, Logan would have to be alert at all times. He didn't believe Hickey had much experience in the woods, but in his current state of mind, Hickey would be more dangerous than ever.

Both men spent the day moving through the woods in search of the other. Neither man had any idea of where the other one was, and the forest was vast. Finding the other may be more luck than skill. Both of them knew it had to end if either was to have another peaceful night's sleep. It had been a long and tiring day, the light was slipping away under the canopy of the trees. Logan built a bed out of pine needles, and after laying down he covered himself with leaves to keep warm and dry. Hickey not being as experienced, merely sat down and leaned up against a tree trunk and went to sleep.

The morning light squirted through the leaves and hit Hickey in the eyes. He woke up cold, and found himself all wet from the evening dew. As much as he wanted to he couldn't risk a fire. He had enough sense to know McCart could smell the smoke and give away his position.

Logan rolled out from underneath the wet leaves that covered him. Although they were wet, they had kept the dew off him, and he was dry and warm. After checking the loads in his pistol, to ensure his powder and percussion caps were dry, his thoughts returned to Hickey. Hopefully he could end it today and prepare to return to his ranch in Kansas. As that thought entered his mind, he thought about his sister, and how happy the two of them had been on the ranch over the last two years.

Hickey and Logan didn't know it, but they had settled down for the night not more than two hundred yards apart from each other. Hickey began moving south, while Logan continued north, unknowingly creating the distance between them.

Logan searched for sign for just over an hour when he decided Hickey wouldn't have gone that far north. Changing directions he headed west. After another fifteen minutes he turned south to head back toward the mine.

The terrain had forced Hickey slightly east. It wasn't long after he had been walking that he found where McCart had stopped for the night. He couldn't believe how close they had been. He picked up McCart's sign headed north, and stopped to consider the situation. Thinking to himself, he thought, *"Eventually, McCart will have to backtrack, and he will pick up my trail. There is no advantage for me to continue any further. I would just keep moving in front him, and then I would be trapped between him and his sidekicks. The terrain will force McCart back this way as it did me."* Hickey looked around for a good place to hide and wait.

Logan picked up Hickey's footprints. It didn't take long to find where he had spent the night. Logan was upset with himself. How could Hickey have been so close and he not know. Based on the direction Hickey was headed, Logan knew Hickey would be forced to travel the route he had come up the mountain. Logan hadn't bothered to cover his overnight bed of pine needles, thinking it wouldn't matter. There was no doubt Hickey would find where he had spent the night. This would give the advantage to Hickey with Logan having to follow the same route.

With the prospect of walking into an ambush, Logan was determined not to make it easy. Instead of following Hickey's tracks, Logan headed down the cliff. He was hoping to get far enough along the ridge to come up behind Hickey. The going was extremely rough. The animal trail he was using wasn't more than eight inches wide. Any misstep could send him tumbling off the cliff.

Hickey was set up behind a stand of bushes keeping a close watch on the trail. He was thinking about his opponent. So far McCart had not made any foolish moves, not that he expected him to. Every time he thought they had killed him, he had somehow survived. As his mind was drifting off and he was thinking of Logan's good fortune, it dawned on him that Logan would not be coming along the trail. He's too smart for that and would find another way. One which would turn the advantage in his favor. He would take the least likely route. Quickly, Hickey moved over to the top of the ridge and look over the side. He was scanning the ridge in every direction, but there was no sign of McCart. He was just turning around to return to the mulberry bushes when the movement caught his eye. There he was, not more that forty yards below him. McCart was holding his body flush to the ridge and inching along, trying not to fall off. The trail he was following was so thin, Hickey couldn't even see it.

Hickey raised his pistol, took careful aim and fired. Logan felt the thud hit his shoulder. He lowered his arm from the pain. But something wasn't right. He glanced over at his shoulder and was surprised to see there wasn't any blood. And while there should have been a searing hot pain, there was only a dull pain where the bullet had hit him. Somehow the bullet had bounced off without penetrating the skin.

Hickey was now talking to himself, *"Damn, I can't believe I missed him."* Hickey fired another shot. The bullet struck right beside Logan, causing him to involuntarily shift his body. When he shifted, he lost his footing and slipped off the trail. He was slamming down the ridge. After several attempts he was able to grab hold of a young sapling and stop his free fall. He was hanging precariously, and if he lost his grip he would fall to his death. The only good thing was that Hickey could no longer see him from up above.

Using the sapling, Logan pulled himself up and was able to lay across a rock jutting out of the cliff. Getting himself into a sitting position he reached down for his pistol. It was gone. Checking the other side he found his knife still in its sheath.

As a child growing up and playing with his Cheyenne and Arapaho blood brothers, Logan had become very skilled with the knife. So much so, that he could kill as quickly and deadly with it, as he could a gun. He would have preferred to still have his pistol, but it wasn't something that would stop him from completing his task.

Logan knew he was in a bad predicament, but there had to be a way out. There almost always is if you can keep your wits about you and think it through.

As hard as he tried, Hickey couldn't see where McCart had fallen. Even if he didn't actually kill him with his shots, the fall most certainly killed him. But Hickey had made that mistake twice before. This time he had to make certain McCart was dead. He couldn't just think him dead. Hickey headed south down the mountain. Once he reached the valley floor, he followed the cliff along the bottom to find McCart's body.

Logan was scouring the side of the cliff for a way down. As he was searching, he thought back to the bullet that had hit him. He figured the shot to be slightly less than fifty yards, and while that is a long shot for a pistol, it still should have penetrated. Playing it back in his mind, he remembered the report of the shots having a dull sound to them. Even in the heavily forested terrain, the shots should have been crisp, and the shots should have had more of a crack to them. To his own astonishment he said the words out loud. "They're wet. There was a heavy dew last night and his cartridges got wet." Powder loses its strength when it gets wet. Sometimes it won't ignite at all. The wet powder reduced the force of the bullets.

While replaying the event in his mind Logan took stock of his injuries from the fall. Other than some ripped clothing, and minor cuts and bruises, he had come through the fall in pretty good condition. One of his boot heels had been ripped off, so using his knife he pried off the other heel. Understanding the leather soles would be to slick for climbing. He tied his socks together and slipped them through the pull tabs of his boots. Then he tied them together and slung them around his neck.

Logan had focused his attention on finding a way down the cliff. It seemed hopeless. Leaning back and tilting his head up, he noticed a string of rocks that could be used to get to the top. It would be difficult because most of them would only allow for a finger or toe hold, but his choices were limited. Carefully he got to his feet and stood up on the rock he was using as a perch. Reaching for the first rock it was just out of his reach. He wasn't sure if the rock he was standing on would support his weight if he missed and dropped back down. Bending at the knees he leapt up, grabbing the small rock above and holding on with his fingers. As he jumped, the rock he had been resting gave away. It was more coal than hard rock. Pulling his legs up at the knees, he gripped his toes to a vine running along the cliff. Pressing to a stand with his toes, he was able to reach up and grab another rock with his hands. Now he was working his way up, switching his hands and feet from rock to rock. Near the top he was assisted by some young saplings. Twice he lost his grip and almost fell to his death. The going was slow and hard, forcing him stop and rest several times. The climb had been hard on his hands and feet, which were raw from the difficult climb. It took about two hours, but he reached the top.

Had Hickey looked up to the top of the ridge when he arrived at the spot he thought Logan had fell. He would have seen Logan crawling over the top of the ridge. But he had kept his focus at the base of the ridge searching for McCart's body.

Logan laid on his back, catching his breath, and regaining his strength. Feeling refreshed and with his breathing back to normal, he slipped his socks and boots back on and started for the mine. He picked up Hickey's tracks headed back down the mountain. He had to get back to the mine to save Charlie and Gideon. He had no idea Hickey had back tracked into the canyon to find his body to confirm he was dead.

Frustrated, that he couldn't find any evidence of Logan's dead body. Hickey was pleased at the fact that there was no evidence McCart had walked away. The only thing he found was McCart's hat and gun. He searched the side of the cliff one more time with his spy glass. He saw no way of escape from the cliff. If McCart is up there and alive, he wouldn't last the night from being shot and the fall. Hickey headed back to the mine. He felt comfortable that McCart was dead, and didn't give him another thought.

Both men were on a path that would take them to the same point in the valley. Each one had his thoughts on what he would do when he arrived back at the mine.

They both stepped into the clearing at the same time. They were no more than twenty paces apart. Hickey drew his pistol as Logan drew his knife. Hickey heard the click of the hammer hit the chamber. The sound of the misfire caught his ears as the knife sank deep into his chest.

Logan walked over and looked down at Hickey lying on the ground with his knife sticking out of Hickey's chest. Hickey made one last effort, raising his pistol he pulled the trigger, only to have another misfire. Looking up into Logan's eyes,

Hickey said, "I don't understand, you should be dead."

"You let your powder get wet last night. You should have re-loaded fresh charges." Hickey's eyes glassed over as he died realizing his fatal mistake.

Epilog

Logan walked out of the trees and into the clearing. Charlie and Gideon were speaking with Mr. Youngblood. It was Charlie who noticed him first and ran over to help him. Logan sat down on a rock while telling them what happened, and that Hickey was dead.

Mr. Youngblood and a couple of his men had rode over to inspect the mine the day before. After finding Charlie and Gideon hidden in the rocks, he decided to stay and help. They found the horses and mules on their way in and brought them back, Dusty had returned on his own.

After another day's rest, they all packed up and headed into Tin Cup. All total, the gold they had mined amounted to one million two hundred thousand dollars. Logan gave Gideon Mr. Youngblood's draft for a hundred thousand dollars purchasing the mine. Gideon wanted to split it too, but Logan convinced him that it was his mine, and that none of them would have prospered if not for that.

The Gideon mine became the most productive in the region. Mr. Youngblood sent a message to the McCart ranch releasing Logan from his obligation to re-pay the purchase price. Once again Mr. Youngblood stated his desire for Logan to come work for him.

Logan, Charlie, Gideon, and Randy, returned to Lawrence Kansas together, where they cashed in their bank drafts. Charlie lived out his days in Kansas City, and kept in close contact with the McCart ranch. Gideon traveled west, and opened a dry goods store and saloon north of San Francisco. He sold goods and liquor to the miners of the great California gold rush.

Before returning to the ranch, Logan posted the death's of the Bellows and Hickey gangs with Marshall Brodie. He received a fifteen thousand dollar reward. Logan gave five thousand dollars of the reward money to Randy. Then he deposited the rest into his account along with his share of the money from the mine.

After driving the herd to Wichita for sale, Logan and the ranch hands built a house and barn for Randy. It sat along the Arkansas River on the Circle M Ranch, not far from the McCart house. Randy would live out his days there, and Joey was made ranch foreman.

Lisa and Greg Stevenson were married. Greg sold his law offices and moved out to the ranch. Lisa and Greg continued to manage the ranch as Logan left to travel the western lands.